FIRE AND FAT

A TALE OF THE
LORD OF DARKNESS

FIRE AND FATE

A TALE OF THE
LORD OF DARKNESS

BY SERENA VALENTINO

DISNEY • HYPERION

LOS ANGELES • NEW YORK

First Edition, July 2023
10 9 8 7 6 5 4 3 2 1
FAC-004510-23145
Printed in the United States of America

This book is set in 13-point Garamond 3 LT Pro.
Designed by Phil Buchanan
Library of Congress Control Number: 2023930019
ISBN 978-1-368-07657-9

Reinforced binding

www.DisneyBooks.com

SUSTAINABLE FORESTRY INITIATIVE

Certified Sourcing

www.forests.org
SFI-01681

Logo Applies to Text Stock Only

Dedicated to my managers and champions, David Server and Ray Miller. Eternally grateful for your optimism, honesty, guidance, and sense of humor. Thank you.

FROM THE BOOK OF FAIRY TALES

Hades

The gossamer strings of fate are intricately entangled in the fabric of the Book of Fairy Tales, woven together like a spider's web. And at its center is Hades: the keeper of the dead in his realm; he who has the power to command the stars and direct destinies—much like us, the Odd Sisters, authors of this Book of Fairy Tales. And while we are all connected by death, our bond with Hades is forged by something far more powerful: *fate*.

Before Hades took his throne in the Underworld, he was happy in his role. He was the Giver of Wealth, God of Hidden Treasure, Gold, and All That Lies

Beneath the Earth, including the dead. But even so, he wasn't sinister, or the demon he became; he was passive and the keeper of balance. He wasn't always evil; that was an attribute he acquired with time, loneliness, and despair after many years in his unhappy kingdom.

Hades wanted nothing more than to escape the misery of his new life, but he took his responsibilities seriously. He was loath to leave his throne unattended, and therefore felt trapped in perpetual doom and anguish. Until one day fate intervened in the guise of three witches: Lucinda, Ruby, and Martha.

If you haven't gathered by now that the stories you have been reading are chapters from the Book of Fairy Tales, then you haven't been paying attention. And though we have established that time is nothing more than a human construct, that all timelines move concurrently rather than separately, you are about to learn why: when the old gods were defeated, namely the Titan Cronus, time was forever fractured. Ever since, we witches have not experienced time in a straight line. Sometimes, we lose our thread and release the stories from our Book of Fairy Tales out of sequence. But there is a method to our madness. What is time to the likes of witches and gods, beings who have the power to create or break worlds, and to direct the cosmos? The only thing we can't control, it would seem, is our own fates.

CHAPTER I

FROM THE BOOK OF FAIRY TALES

Brothers of War

When we read about myths and legends, it is easy to forget they are not just histories but lived experiences and events that shaped the lives of those involved. We forget that powerful beings, even gods, have their struggles and heartbreaks, and we forget these are not just stories.

The events in this tale took place during a time that is hard for mortals to fathom, when behemoth Titans ruled with fire and chaos until they were eventually overthrown by their sons and daughters, the mighty and powerful Olympians.

The reign of the Titans had become so rife with

pandemonium and destruction, Zeus, Hades, and Poseidon decided it was time to overthrow their father, Cronus, and the other Titans and become the new ruling pantheon of gods. This battle would later be named the War of the Titans, a ten-year war pitting Olympians against Titans, new gods against old, children against fathers. A war marked by such heroism it found its way into the pages of our Book of Fairy Tales, so epic its reverberations were felt throughout the realms, including the Many Kingdoms. A war that helped shape Hades into the god he is today.

Hades was a major figure in this battle, and he and his brothers knew if they were going to overthrow the Titans, they would need the greatest of armies to defeat them. Titans were not mere giants; they were eaters of worlds, and larger than any mountain. The brothers knew they had to call upon every power at their disposal if they were to rule in the Titans' stead. And that is what they did.

Poseidon called upon the sea, summoning great waves that carried all manner of sea creatures into the fray. Giant squids, monstrous octopuses, and even the great leviathans joined the fight. The creatures wrapped their strong tentacles around the Titans, holding them in place as they were enveloped by violently crashing waves. On those waves sailed moldering and decaying ships filled with armies of the dead reanimated by Hades's power. Seas of skeletons stood on these ships, on every mountaintop, on every field, and astride Zeus's fleet of giant eagles. Zeus hurled his thunderbolts from above, commanding the sky to bring down torrential rains and winds more powerful than the strongest of hurricanes. If the Titans threw mountains at Hades's army, he would simply raise them again, sending the poor souls to their doom again and again. A death swarm enveloped the Titans as they fought off foes from every direction. For ten years the brothers fought together as one, side by side, until finally the Titans were defeated and locked away.

On the final day of the battle against the Titans, a decision was made that would shape all of their fates, and indeed the fate of the worlds. Hades could see it was already in the making the moment the war ended. Hades spied his brothers among the ruins of their war; wrecked ships littered the landscape, buildings were crumbled, pillars were cracked, temples were submerged in water, and he wondered what Zeus and Poseidon were discussing. Even though Hades was the eldest son of the Titan Cronus, Zeus always took the lead, and Hades could feel Zeus was already deciding how things would go now that their father, Cronus, was locked away like the other Titans.

Hades dismounted his giant three-headed dog, Cerberus, and looked at his brothers with a sly glint in his eye. He could see what was happening. It was written on their faces, just as it was written by fate.

"Of course you shall rule the sea, my brother," Zeus said, patting Poseidon on the back. "And Hades here shall rule the Underworld." Zeus's smile was broad, flashing his large white teeth.

"And I suppose you will rule the sky and everything that comes with it, including Olympus?" asked Hades, feeling himself become hot with anger. Cerberus narrowed his eyes and growled at Zeus.

"Why? Did you have something else in mind, Hades?" asked Zeus, scratching one of Cerberus's heads under the chin, and giving each head a tasty severed tentacle.

"I am the eldest son, Zeus. It should be me! And stop trying to butter up my dog!"

"Let's not forget: if it weren't for me, you'd still be living in the belly of our father, Hades. Our sisters and brother haven't forgotten."

"Yes, yes, we all know you're the only one Father didn't eat, and you made him—"

"Regurgitate you," said Zeus, laughing. "And you were the last, Hades. So in a way, you're the youngest."

"I was . . . expelled . . . last because I was the firstborn, and I was Dad's favorite!" All of this was true, of course, but that didn't matter to Zeus. Hades knew he shouldn't have been surprised this was happening. From the moment Zeus freed his siblings from the depths of their father's stomach, he acted as if he were the eldest son, with all the privileges that came along with it.

"Just because I masterfully commanded the dead

doesn't mean I want to live with them! I should have a say where I reside for eternity," said Hades feeling the heat of his anger rising within him. He had never felt that way before, the stifling heat, the burning, as if he were being consumed by fire, until finally his body exploded into flames, scorching everything around him. Zeus simply smirked and shook his head.

"That settles it, then. It's clear we're all suited to our roles. I shall rule the sky; Poseidon, the sea; and Hades, the Underworld. Unless there are any objections, *Hades*? You're welcome, of course, to release the Titans and see if you're still Dad's favorite. We could have another ten-year war." What is ten years to a god? But the truth was, Hades didn't want to fight his brother, at least not then. So he agreed to rule the Underworld for the sake of peace, and for family. How bad could it be?

And this was how Hades was made the lord of the Underworld. But that was not the end of Hades's story. It was only the beginning.

CHAPTER II

THE BREAKING OF THE WORLDS

The worlds have been broken many times: by the gods, and by witches, and by blundering humans dabbling in magic they didn't understand. This was the day the worlds broke so violently even the god Hades didn't know if he could repair them. But as you will soon learn, Hades was the only being who could put things right, because he tangled our fates together, binding us in ways we never thought possible. If you have read the other stories from the Book of Fairy Tales, you know this wasn't Hades's first visit to the Many Kingdoms. But it was the first time

Hazel and Primrose would make his acquaintance, hundreds of years after his first visit to the Many Kingdoms, and longer still after he took the throne in the Underworld

On that day, Hazel and Primrose stood in the courtyard in the shadow of the ancient stone mansion that was perched on the tallest hill in the Dead Woods, contemplating the history of their kingdom and the events that made them queens of this land.

The Queens of the Dead had ruled this realm for longer than time itself. Before Hazel and Primrose's reign, the queens of the Dead Woods were known for their cruelty and unfathomable necromantic powers. They demanded all the dead from the surrounding villages be buried in their kingdom so that they might take dominion over them. Those who didn't comply with their demands were slaughtered and brought into the undead ranks of the Dead Woods. The queens' necromantic powers and secrets of extraordinary long life were passed down to each new generation, mothers to daughters. The lore is steeped in blood and trauma, and the kingdom remained a bleak and deathly place until Hazel and Primrose, daughters of the previous queen, took their place as rulers in the haunted realm.

Hundreds of years prior, Hazel and Primrose lived in the Dead Woods as children with their sister Gothel, and their mother, Manea, Queen of the Dead. When they all came of age, they were expected to accept their mother's blood so her power would be passed down to them. When Hazel and Primrose refused, their mother tried to force it upon them, giving Gothel no choice but to kill her own mother. So the Wraith Queen Manea took revenge on Primrose and Hazel, killing them and leaving Gothel alone, desperate to find a way to bring her sisters back from the dead. For many years, even after Gothel's death, Primrose and Hazel slept the sleep of the dead, until one day they were revived and made their way back to the only home they knew, the Dead Woods. There, they became friends and allies with Circe, and joined her in the fight against her mothers, Lucinda, Ruby, and Martha, who wanted to rule the Dead Woods and bring darkness and terror to all the realms. The Odd Sisters were so deranged at this point they had lost all sense of reason, and their hearts were only filled with hate. It had been a slow process bringing them to this state, but it seemed their madness had been fated from the beginning.

When the Odd Sisters were much younger, they had a little sister named Circe, whom they loved more than anything. She was their everything, their shining star, their greatest love, and they held her even more dear than their own lives. One day she was tragically taken from them in a heartbreaking accident, the day Maleficent turned into a dragon and burned the Fairylands in a fit of rage and sorrow. The Odd Sisters didn't blame Maleficent, but in their grief they made it their mission to create another sister by devising a spell that would use the best parts of themselves. They used old and dangerous magic created by the Queens of the Dead, magic to create daughters. And that is what they did; they created a daughter from blood and magic, without knowing it would slowly erode everything that was good within them, eventually turning them mad. But they had their Circe back, and they called her sister rather than daughter, and never told her the truth of her origins.

Then one day, many years later, Circe, with the help of Snow White, learned what the Odd Sisters had done.

Circe learned the Odd Sisters had given too much of themselves in the creation of her, and it had turned them into fiendish witches just as vile as the Queens of the Dead. Circe felt she had no other choice than to sacrifice herself, in hopes it would return to the Odd Sisters what they had lost in creating her.

And through this act the Odd Sisters and Circe went to the Place Between (the living and the dead), where Circe could keep watch on her mothers until she decided what to do.

It had been several weeks since Circe took her own life to save all of theirs, and Hazel and Primrose waited in hope that Circe would return to them, but as more time passed, they started to lose faith and slipped further into despair. Hazel and Primrose were now left with nothing but their own grief.

The Dead Woods felt even lonelier now that Snow White had gone home to her own kingdom. Circe and Snow were cousins, good friends, and the best of companions. She stood alongside Circe, Primrose, and Hazel during the battle with the Odd Sisters, and mourned Circe's death profoundly. But there was nothing Snow could do to bring her friend back, no matter how much love she had in her heart, or how many tears she shed. She was needed back at home with her family, so after a tearful goodbye, she pulled away in her carriage, promising to write Primrose and Hazel as soon as she reached her own kingdom. When Primrose and Hazel watched Snow's carriage pull out from the courtyard amongst the weeping angels and ancient crypts, their sorrow swept over them like a torrent.

They had lost Circe, and now Snow White was on her way home. Feeling their losses deeply, Hazel and Primrose thought the entirety of the Dead Woods shared in their sorrow. Even the gorgon statue near the fountain under the mossy oak and the stone creatures perched on the massive mansion seemed to be weeping that day, while the caws from the crows in the branches of the newly blossoming trees sang a song of grief.

"Hazel, look at this," said Primrose. "The trees are showing their colors, and the moss is green rather than gray. How is that possible?" Her eyes sparkled with wonder and just the hint of happiness on this sad day.

"This may be a place for the dead, but it needn't be a dead place." Hazel's words reminded Primrose of the waking dream she'd had about a mysterious man named James who visited them in the Dead Woods. He flashed in her mind just as vividly as he had originally appeared, and she wondered if the dream hadn't been a vision of something that would come to pass, but she was too distracted just then, realizing the meaning of Hazel's words.

"You did this? With your magic? Why didn't I think of that?" Primrose looked around at the green leaves and tiny colorful blooms in the trees. It reminded her of when they were children and she would tie ribbons with colorful hearts on the decayed tree branches. It had been her way of bringing color and life into the dead place. It made her heart happy to realize they had the power to alter the Dead Woods however they wished. They were the Queens of the Dead now, and she felt for the first time that she would be happy there. And she was more convinced than ever that her waking dream was a glimpse into the future.

"Circe would love this," Primrose said with a wave of her hand, and the red blooms grew bigger and more vibrant. The color of blood. Then, suddenly, the memory of Circe's gruesome death flashed in her mind with a violence that sent pain throughout her entire body. "I can't get the image of Circe's death out of my mind. I think it's going to haunt me forever. But, Hazel, I have a strange feeling she is coming home—do you think that's possible?"

"I'm not sure. Taking her own life stopped her mothers from destroying this land and countless others. The Odd Sisters seem happy in the Place

Between, themselves again, but I'm not sure if Circe will be able to talk them into going beyond the veil. I don't know what's going to happen."

Primrose didn't seem convinced. "I don't know, Hazel. I think I had a vision of the future. We were all laughing together, you, me, and Circe; we were chatting with a strange and charming man who traveled from across the sea to bring us an enormous cake, and we couldn't stop laughing." Primrose was laughing now, even at the thought of it. This man with his unusual but dashing clothing, a flashy mustache, and an unmistakably good heart.

"I'm sure it was you who couldn't stop laughing. But why would he travel all that way just to bring us a cake?" asked Hazel.

"It was a really big cake! But there was more to it. Circe asked him to stay in the Dead Woods— we all did—but we couldn't convince him to stay. Everything was so different in my vision, the rapunzel flowers were everywhere, scattered across the Many Kingdoms, and the Dead Woods were filled with so much life. Even Mrs. Tiddlebottom was young again.

Maybe we should look at the Book of Fairy Tales and see if it's true. I think the man's name was James. Maybe his story is on our shelves."

Hazel sighed. "I thought you were afraid to look in the book. As a rule, we don't read stories that haven't happened yet."

"Circe says one day we will see time the way she does, all at once, and I think it's starting to happen to me now with these visions. Why not take a look? Besides, we found James delightful, and reading his story might be a lovely diversion." Primrose always counted on her optimism to be infectious, which it often was, but Hazel wasn't budging.

"She also says she keeps herself tethered to one timeline so she doesn't lose her mind. Perhaps we should just wait and see what happens. It can be something to look forward to."

Primrose wondered if her sister was right. "Come on, Hazel. We're witches. We're supposed to know the future. What will it hurt? If we had read all of the stories about Circe in the Book of Fairy Tales, she might still be alive. She might be with us right now!"

"Or things could be a lot worse. Come on, let's go back inside and have a cup of tea and a slice of Snow's gooseberry pie. She made more pies than we could possibly eat, because you said you loved them so much." This made Primrose smile. She had grown to love Snow and missed her already, even though she had just left. At least she had her pies.

As Primrose and Hazel were about to make their way back inside, they were distracted by a blinding pale blue light, so bright they were sure it could be seen all around the Many Kingdoms. The light took the shape of a swirling blue vortex, blazing like a hot flame, causing everything in the Dead Woods to stir and the dead within their graves to wake from their slumber.

One by one the dead emerged from their crypts and from under the ground where they slept, brushing the dirt and dust from their clothes and squinting against the sunlight in their eyes. It had been years since Primrose and Hazel laid eyes on the army of the dead at their disposal. Not since the time of their mother had they been summoned in this way, and the two women didn't understand what power was springing them to life once more. For centuries the queens before them had been hoarding a legion of dead beneath them, and now these poor souls were standing before Primrose and Hazel, their queens, silently awaiting their command. But Hazel and Primrose didn't understand why.

Their manservant, their protector and champion, their dearest friend, Jacob—once raised from the dead himself—entered the garden and watched the dead coming to life before them.

"Jacob, what's going on? Why is this happening?" But Primrose could see by the look on Jacob's face that he didn't know, either.

Like most witches, Primrose could read minds, and she heard Jacob's thoughts. He was panic-stricken. He feared the Odd Sisters had found their way out of the Place Between and had come back to destroy them.

Primrose felt terrible for Jacob, for everything he experienced over the years in the name of loyalty to the Queens of the Dead, and she could see it was taking a toll on him. One day she would read his story in the Book of Fairy Tales. She was sure there was more to his tale besides what was documented in the chapter dedicated to the Odd Sisters, but that would be a good place to begin.

"Don't worry, Jacob. This is not the Odd Sisters' magic. I do not feel them among us." Primrose squinted against the bright light of the vortex as a form began to emerge from within. No, this was someone entirely unexpected. Someone far more powerful. As the form took shape, and shifted into focus, they suddenly knew who this legendary god was. He appeared uncharacteristically silent and solemn, his eyes blazing yellow against pale blue skin. His cloak swirled in plumes of smoke that moved like tentacles, stretching out like a great smoldering leviathan. His hair blazed blue fire, and in his arms was Circe, her skin glowing blue from the light of the vortex behind them.

"Circe!" Hazel's gray eyes flashed as she rushed toward Circe, Primrose following close behind her. Hades grinned at the witches as he gingerly draped

Circe's body on the marble steps of a nearby crypt. Her long red gown swayed in the current of the vortex like waves of blood.

"I wasn't expecting such a deliciously gruesome welcome," Hades said, gesturing to the endless rows of dead assembled in the courtyard, reaching all the way back through the woods to the tall rosebush thicket that surrounded their kingdom. The dead stared at Hades with hollow eyes; they were not sparking with life like the eyes of Sir Jacob, who took his place between Primrose and Hazel and grasped them each by the hand like a protective father. They had never met Hades, but the lord of the Underworld's reputation was well known to them.

"I know it's customary to bring cake to the Dead Woods, but I thought you'd forgive the oversight under the circumstances," Hades said, motioning to Circe. "What I'm bringing is so much better."

"What's happened to Circe? And why did you raise our dead?" Hazel was holding fast to Jacob's hand and Primrose could see she was afraid to rush toward Circe, but she was clearly not too afraid to question this god who had appeared so suddenly in their courtyard.

Hades laughed, revealing his rictus smile and sharp dagger teeth. "I have no need to make a display of my power within your kingdom, dear ladies. It is the return of your queen here who brings the dead to life. But I would be happy to add to the splendor of this auspicious occasion." He raised his hands and stretched them skyward, like a dramatic stage actor about to recite the greatest of soliloquies.

"All hail Queen Circe, our divine ruler of the Dead Woods . . ." His booming voice rang out, but before he could continue, something distracted him. Annoyed by the interruption, he directed his attention to the distraction. Glowing spirits of the previous queens of the Dead Woods were rising from the earth, floating through the trees and in and out of their branches. They circled the endless graves and the statues that adorned them, then rose to the heights of the mansion, swirling up to the glass solarium. The spirits danced in the gorgon fountain, wove among the legion of the dead, and paused at each gargoyle, raven, and harpy statue as if to say hello, like children happy to see their home again. They danced on the breeze, rejoicing, until finally they landed in the courtyard. The dark queens who once ruled this land—now wraiths made of shadow—stood before Hades, their eyes glowing white and their mouths like black pits. These dark queens spoke to Hades as one, their voices filling the courtyard and making the trees wither and lose their blooms and green foliage with each word they spoke.

"Lord of the Dead, we thank you for returning Circe to us, but you are not welcome here." The sound of the Wraith Queens stirred Circe from her sleep. She sat up and opened her eyes, taking everything in. Once she seemed to realize where she was, she was angry.

"Where are my mothers? How dare you rip me from the Place Between!" She tried to stand but was too unsteady and disoriented.

"Really, not even a thank-you?" Hades said, putting his hand on his hip, his tentacles swishing like the tail of an annoyed cat. "I saved your life, little

25

queen, and if you recall, your mothers are no longer your mothers. They are one mother. Singular. One. Just Lucinda! Remember? You fused them together, and she's angrier than . . . well, me on a bad day!" Hades reached out his hand to help Circe stand, but she didn't take it. She was clearly still angry with Hades for whatever happened in the Place Between. Primrose couldn't glean the events from either of their minds, so she would just have to wait until she could talk to Circe.

"Thank you," Circe said, bracing herself against the angel statue and glaring at Hades as she stood. "I can stand on my own. Tell me, why is a god intervening in the lives of witches? Why bring me here against my will? Why risk breaking the worlds in the process?"

"Because a long time ago I made a deal with your mothers. Years ago, I told them they could have any wish in exchange for something they did for me, and it seems, after all these years, they decided to call in their favor. They wanted you out of the Place Between, so I brought you here. Simple as that. I am a hellion of my word, after all." His smile was friendly, with a bit of cheekiness thrown in for good measure. He was doing his best to be charming. It wasn't a stretch—he *was* charming—but Primrose could see he was, as they say, on his best behavior. "Believe me, little witch, you're better off here where you can stay clear of your mother's wrath until you can decide what you want to do," said Hades, looking around the Dead Woods with a deep sigh, like he was happy to be there.

This was not what Primrose had expected from the lord of the Underworld. She, Circe, and Hazel just stood there blinking at him, trying to take everything in, but before any more could be said, they caught something stirring in their peripheral vision.

It was Lucinda's silhouette in the center of the vortex. Her ringlets were in tangles, and her dark-circled eyes peered at them from her blood-stained face. Her body was oddly misshapen and contorted as she emerged from the swirling blue light on her hands and knees, screaming in agony as her bones audibly cracked and snapped. The Wraith Queens flew to her aid, dragging her through the vortex until finally she lay in a heap at the feet of a massive weeping angel on the other side. The angel looked as if she were protecting Lucinda under the cover of her wings, as Lucinda let out a horrifying chorus of misery, with Ruby's and Martha's voices joining hers, creating an aria of agony. Lucinda writhed in torment as her body violently seized. When she suddenly stopped moving, the Wraith Queens gathered around, whispering in her ears. Fear washed over Primrose and Hazel as Lucinda finally rose to her feet, the Wraith Queens holding up her limp body. She looked like an old doll, broken and lifeless.

"What is happening? What's wrong with her?" Circe cried.

But Hades quickly put himself in front of her as Lucinda's limp body was again infused with rage and lunged at her daughter. Lucinda was clawing and reaching for Circe, but she couldn't get past Hades. He was an unmovable force, too strong even for Lucinda's torrent of anger. "Do you think I would let you harm your daughter after everything you sacrificed to create her?"

But Lucinda didn't answer Hades. She was singularly focused on Circe.

"Look at me!" Lucinda hissed, still trying to grab Circe, locking her eyes on her daughter as she screamed at her. "You did this to me! I am in torment because of you. My sisters are digging their way out of me, clawing at my insides, scratching at my soul, wanting nothing more than to escape my body! The prison you put them in! All so they can kill *you*!"

"I didn't mean for this to happen, I swear."

"Do not pretend you didn't wish for this." The Wraith Queens' faces were full of rage as the wind whipped around them. *"You are not the first daughter of the Dead Woods to betray their mother,"* they said as they swirled around everyone in the courtyard, lashing at their faces and whispering incantations on the wind.

"And I am not the first mother to destroy her daughter!" Lucinda's voice was full of purpose as she raised her hands, causing a shock wave of power and sending the Wraith Queens' spirits to disperse into black dust, which scattered throughout the Dead Woods.

"You vile hags! I didn't ask for your help. Withdraw from this place at once and leave my daughter to me!" said Lucinda, raising her arms in declaration. "Hear my words! I will break the worlds and watch my wretched daughter languish in despair as she witnesses the destruction of everyone and everything she holds dear! I will see the destruction of this kingdom before I give it over to these usurpers, these impostor witches, these so-called Queens of the Dead! All will suffer in my wake and know the true meaning of despair."

Hades rolled his eyes theatrically and clapped. "Wow, that was quite a speech. Do you think we can move this along with a little less monologuing? I've had enough of Greek tragedies, if you know what I mean."

"How dare you! You side with Circe, after everything my sisters and I have done for you? You have meddled with our lives for the last time, devil! Not even you can keep her safe from me!"

"That's enough!" said Hades, grabbing Lucinda by her disheveled ringlets and effortlessly tossing her through the vortex, closing it with the snap of his fingers.

"And I thought my family was bad!" he said. "I had no idea how Shakespearean your mothers had become."

They all looked at him, puzzled.

"Come on now, the *Scottish play*? Everyone knows about the witches in the *Scottish play*. Or is that too far after your time? I thought witches saw all time at once. Not there yet? Never mind. It's refreshing, really, I really hate a know-it-all, anyway," Hades said, wiping the blood off his robes. "I'd say it's time for introductions. Of course, you know who I am! I am the legendary lord of the dead. And I had the pleasure of meeting Circe in the Place Between before Lucinda demanded I take her away. I take it you're the famous Primrose and Hazel? Come, isn't anyone going to offer me some tea? The hospitality in these lands is legendary, and I think I could use some after all that drama."

The queens of the Dead Woods didn't know what to make of Hades; he wasn't at all as they expected. But they did know one thing: they were curious to hear what he was doing there.

Chapter III

The Return of the Queen

Hades, Primrose, and Hazel sat in the solarium while they waited for Circe to join them. Jacob had escorted Circe to her chambers so she could collect herself while Primrose and Hazel served the lord of the Underworld some tea, as he requested.

Atop the ancient stone mansion, the solarium shined like a sparkling jewel against the purple twilight, slowly fading into black. Jacob was now down below, preparing for the lighting of the Dead Woods to honor their royal guest while Hades and the witches sipped their tea. Their view was awe-inspiring, and Hades couldn't help but feel the magic that emanated from this dark and foreboding place. This was one of the few kingdoms he hadn't visited properly during his time in the Many Kingdoms, and he was pleased to have finally breached the formidable fortress to take tea with the Queens of the Dead at last. Queens who were by all accounts much more welcoming than their predecessors.

He watched as some of the undead minions below made their way back to their graves, ushered by Jacob, an interesting man—or what was left of the man he once was. For a being who was mainly bone and thick, leathery skin, he cut quite the figure under his ancient soldier's uniform. He didn't strike Hades as fully human, that is, not even fully human before he became undead. His bones were unusually large, and he was much taller than the average man. Hades could tell he had been handsome when he was alive, and he could sense both his strength and his compassion. He was the legendary Sir Jacob who still served the queens of the Dead Woods after all these years, always there to help, guide, and council the new, inexperienced queens, as had been his lot for more years than even he could recollect. It seemed to Hades that Jacob was the real person in charge of this kingdom. Hades made sure to veil these thoughts from the witches, though he had a feeling he might have to take special care to keep his thoughts from Circe; she was by far the most powerful witch he had ever encountered, at least since her mothers.

"There is nothing quite like a nice cup of tea in the Many Kingdoms. I can't tell you how many times I've been tempted over the years to pop over for a cup, and you know, I think I might just do that now that Maleficent is no longer squatting in my old castle. And thank the gods that horrible Fairy Godmother is no longer bumbling about shouting orders at everyone. I knew it would only be a matter of time before her sister, Nanny, put her in her place!" Hades laughed between bites of cake and sips of tea. He enjoyed being in the company of witches again, and drinking their tea from a cup he was sure the Odd Sisters had taken from his dining hall many years before. Anyone who knew the Odd Sisters with any intimacy knew they had a stash of teacups they

34

had taken from their various friends, family, foes, and acquaintances.

"You know the fairies?" asked Primrose. She smiled, making her freckle-splashed nose crinkle in a way Hades thought was adorable. Hades had a soft spot for witches, especially witches such as these. Powerful witches who didn't talk in riddles, and who weren't unhinged or know-it-alls like the Fates; he detested almost nothing more than a know-it-all. He liked these witches because, like him, they understood what it was to be keepers of the dead. And he thought they were a delight, Hazel with her gray, thoughtful eyes that took everything in and filed it away in case she would need it again, and Primrose with her inner light and desire to transform her kingdom into something beautiful: both of them more powerful than they knew. These were rare witches, and Hades was happy to be in their company. He was already enamored with them, just as he had been with the Odd Sisters so many years ago. But these witches, they were easier to love. Easier to talk to and spend time with. If he hadn't already learned his lesson from the last time he visited the Many Kingdoms, he would happily spend the rest of his days with these witches in the Dead Woods. But fate had other plans for Hades.

"Oh, Fairy Godmother and I go way back, though I don't think she'd admit it," he said with a flourish of his hand and a glint in his eyes. He motioned to a skeleton minion nearby for another cup of tea, then continued talking.

"I still feel the spirits of the Queens of the Dead in the room with us now, hovering and fretting, but I assure you, I have no intention of taking up residence in the Many Kingdoms again, nor of showing a display of my power in your lands. I owed the Odd Sisters a favor, and I granted it; that is all I came here to do. But I couldn't stand by and watch Lucinda kill her daughter after everything she and her sisters went through to create her," he said while munching apple caramel tarts, quickly brushing away the crumbs from his robes when he heard someone come into the solarium.

"And what do you know of that, Lord of the

Dead?" Circe stood in the arched doorway. She had changed into a long silver gown that shined like moonlight. Hades could see the joy in Hazel's and Primrose's hearts to see Circe again.

"I know more than I'd care to admit," said Hades.

"And the Wraith Queens? Do you know why they appeared? I've never known them to side with my mother," said Circe, making her way to sit on the red velvet divan with Primrose and Hazel across from where Hades sat in the window seat.

"I'm afraid that is my fault, too. I promised them I would never set foot in this land, and I broke that promise to keep another," said Hades.

"I thought they were safely beyond the veil. Are you telling me they can enter the land of the living anytime they wish?" asked Hazel, who looked weary, and Hades knew his reply would not console her.

"All too easily, if disturbed. But these are things you should already know. Things it seems you will have to discover on your own, if you want to rule this land." Hades realized he was taking a fatherly role with these witches already, thinking of reasons to stay. But he had made that mistake once before with other witches, and it had been disastrous; he wasn't going to do it again. So he changed the subject. "But you are safe for now, and I am happy to see you looking so well. It's a tragedy the little queen Snow White isn't still here to welcome you home, Circe. I feel her sorrow heavily in the air, drifting around us, mingling with the many wraiths that haunt this place, though of course Snow White is still very much alive. She will be overjoyed to learn you are home again. You must send her a raven the moment you can," he said, taking the slice of pie the skeleton servant handed him. Hades felt quite at ease in the Dead Woods. He had always had a fondness for the Many Kingdoms, but being in the Dead Woods was like being home, only with much more delightful company.

Hades thought there was nothing quite like being in the company of fine witches. Circe was everything he had imagined she would be. What else could she be but brilliant when she possessed the best parts of three of the most powerful witches in history? She surpassed even the original Circe, in Hades's eyes, but that was another story. For another time and place.

"You realize your abilities are even more powerful than your mothers', so let's hope the next time Lucinda goes all Macbeth on you, you won't hesitate to put an end to her madness. And you can always call me if you need help. It wouldn't be the first time I was summoned by witches," he said, motioning for another slice of pie from the skeleton servant, who stood near a long table that was covered with plates of cookies and pies and cakes, and pots of different types of tea sitting upon magical flames that kept them warm.

"And how would we contact you?" asked Circe, narrowing her eyes at Hades as he got up and lifted all the lids off the various teapots, sniffing them to see which he'd like next.

"One of your mothers' magic mirrors, of course. I had two of them, actually, but I think I left one behind in the Forbidden Mountain. I hope Maleficent made good use of it," he said, taking the pie from the skeletal creature who had been waiting for him to select which tea he would like before handing it to him.

"By the gods, this is the most delicious pie I have ever had. We don't have pie in the Underworld—or ice cream. Did you know that? It's a travesty, a crime! Just one of the many injustices I must endure. I forgot how many delectable things there are to eat in this land. I appreciate you indulging me. Honestly, I just wanted to satisfy myself that the new Queens of the Dead were up to their duties, something I would have been obliged to do even if we weren't already tangled in the same strings of fate. And, of course, there is the matter of offering my sincerest apology, and my help, if you will take it. And that, ladies, is something I rarely do, so please, let's not spread it around."

"What is it that you rarely do, Hades, apologize or help?"

And Hades laughed, realizing Circe had a bit of her mothers' wit after all.

"Well, both to be honest, but I meant apologize. You see, I am the reason the Odd Sisters are so, *you know* . . . so . . . *Odd Sistery.*"

The party moved their gathering into the library. The ladies rarely spent time there, though it was one of the most beautiful rooms in the mansion. Hades sat on the massive stone love seat adorned with carved ravens, his hand resting on one of the ravens' heads as his long spectral robe writhed contentedly on the gray stone floor.

Circe was sitting in a chair to the left of the stone fireplace; above it was a portrait of her mothers when they were still young women. She deliberately sat there so the painting would be at her back because when she faced it, she felt like their eyes were upon her, chastising her for what she had done to them. The fireplace was flanked by two large crows carved from black marble—or perhaps it was onyx, Circe now couldn't recall, but she loved them and felt warmed by the purple blazing fire that made the room look as if they were in perpetual twilight. Primrose and Hazel were curled up in their favorite

41

window seat, a reading nook that looked out on the courtyard. Primrose was waving her hand toward the courtyard, making the grounds burst with colorful blooms again, bigger and brighter than they were before the Wraith Queens made them wither. Hazel had her eyes fixed on Hades as she elbowed Primrose, a reminder that they had an honored guest to entertain, though Hades didn't seem to mind.

Circe thought Hades looked quite at home in this older part of the mansion, with its stone carvings of dragons, harpies, and gargoyles. The skeletal minions had placed candles on almost every surface of the room and lit the chandeliers overhead, while others were in the courtyard being directed by Sir Jacob. The room smelled of flowers wafting in from the large double doors that were open to the courtyard, and she was happy to be home. She had forgotten how lovely this room was, with its stone ravens perched on the bookshelves and the candlelight dancing around the room like wistful ghosts. She loved the ancient stonework, the intricate carvings, and the lavish tapestries that hung on the walls on either side of the fireplace. She wondered which of the queens had picked them out, and then she remembered it was Nestis who had a fondness for dragons and the color red, so she reasoned it must have been her.

At Hades's request, Circe asked one of their skeleton servants to arrange for more tea and baked treats to be brought into the library and set out on little round tables. There were a number of their skeleton minions milling around the house at the ready should the party need anything. Circe wondered how it made Primrose and Hazel feel to see the mansion and the grounds filled with skeletal servants like in the days when their mother ruled as queen in the Dead Woods. Those were terrible, dark days that still haunted the witches, and Circe was wary of causing anyone more pain. She wanted to ask them if they were okay and what had happened after she and her mothers went to the Place Between. She wanted to ask after Snow White, and to know how Nanny and Tulip were. And Pflanze and Mrs. Tiddlebottom, they had been in the Place Between with Circe and Lucinda when Hades reached in and brought her out.

What happened to them? She wanted to know everything. And then she realized she could, if she wished, know everything in a single instant. But she'd rather hear it from Hazel and Primrose, and she would, once Hades was no longer in attendance.

Hades was eyeing the bookshelves as if he were looking for something in particular. He seemed completely at ease in their company. He wasn't what Circe had been expecting when she read about the king of the Underworld. She had imagined someone like the former Queens of the Dead: tyrannical, bloodthirsty, and unhinged. Hades seemed charming and kind, but not afraid to use his powers when needed. She felt there was much she could learn from him. She saw Hades smile and knew he was reading her thoughts, but she didn't mind.

"Don't worry, my queen, both Pflanze and Mrs. Tiddlebottom are quite safe, and I assure you, I won't outstay my welcome. At least, I will endeavor not to."

"I do hope you can at least stay long enough for the lighting of the Dead Woods, Lord Hades. Sir Jacob is preparing for it now." Primrose looked positively giddy at the idea. Circe could see Hades was delighted by Primrose, and who wouldn't be? She was their bright star, their shining light, always bursting with love and hope.

"I wouldn't miss it. I like Jacob very much, though he's not said a word to me since I arrived. I know his story, of course, and who he is to you. His bravery and loyalty are legendary."

Circe smiled, hearing Hades say these words. He had to know he was endearing himself to them, spellbinding them with his kind words about Jacob. She had to wonder if he was truly being sincere, or if this was all an act.

"How do you know so much about us?" Circe wondered, not meaning to say it aloud.

"Your mothers. And the Book of Fairy Tales, of course. I think you should read it—all of it, I mean, and the numerous spell books and tomes in this place. There are measures, for example, you can take to keep those wraith hags locked away. There is still so much for you to learn. Speaking of which, what, if anything, did your mothers tell you about my time in the Many Kingdoms?" he asked, taking another sip of tea and scanning the bookshelves again.

"Almost nothing at all," said Circe, wondering what Hades was looking for.

"Well then, it's about time you hear my story. It's a good one, I assure you. It *is* about me, after all. And I could tell you myself—usually I'd jump at the chance—but I think I'd rather just sit here eating these delicious cookies and drinking your splendid tea while we let the Odd Sisters tell it themselves. And perhaps in the telling of it, I will appear more like you expected. But we all change, Circe. Even gods," he said, piling cherry almond cookies on the edge of his tea saucer and inspecting his cup with a critical gaze. "I am going to take this cup and saucer back to the Underworld with me. I hope you don't mind."

"We don't mind at all. But what do you mean by letting my mothers tell the story 'themselves'?" Circe turned to look at the portrait of her mothers hanging over the fireplace, and just for a moment she had to wonder if it was a trick of the light and shadow, or if she really saw their eyes move to meet hers. She had the most foreboding feeling that Lucinda would find her way out of the Place Between again, and Circe wouldn't have the strength to stand against her. Circe had always felt like there was something holding her back, and she knew it was more than just her love for her mothers.

"Oh, there is a reason for that, Circe. And it's bound in part of a promise I made to Pflanze," said Hades, reading her mind.

"Pflanze? What promise?" she asked, turning away again from the portrait of her mothers and focusing on Hades.

"It's all in the Book of Fairy Tales. I assumed that's why you brought us to the library. It's right there on the shelf. You're going to love this! I'm surprised your mothers didn't teach you this little trick. All you have to do is tap the book three times, and it's magically read aloud by its authors," he said. And with a wave of his hand, the book flew toward him and landed on his lap.

"Everything you need to know is here in the Book of Fairy Tales. And it's not just *our* stories and secrets on these pages, but their own. Your mothers are dangerous, Circe, far more than I realized, far more than I feared. We have to do something, and I want you to let me help you."

"They are my responsibility, not yours. I am the reason they went mad. This is my fault, not yours."

"Oh, I think it *is* my fault. That is why you need to hear my story," he said as the book on his lap opened magically, its pages flipping until he found the chapter he was trying to locate.

"One day, we won't have to use magic in order to listen to books, can you imagine?" he said, waiting for a reaction, but the witches just looked at him suspiciously.

"Really? Nothing? Fine. Let's have a listen, then," he said, tapping the book three times with his fingers.

CHAPTER IV

FROM THE BOOK OF FAIRY TALES

The King of the Underworld

After the War of the Titans, Hades was cast away to live with the dead, languishing in the Underworld, dreaming of his life before he and his brothers defeated and locked away the old gods. While he had to admit the world was better off without the Titans, his life was not. He was deeply discontented, and he envied his brothers, Zeus and Poseidon, and the other Olympians, who all seemed happy in their new roles, while Hades hated being lord of the Underworld. To say it was a dreary place was an understatement. He regretted not standing up to Zeus the day they divided the realms. Hades was the eldest brother, and he felt he deserved to rule Olympus, but Zeus always seemed to get his way. Just because he had flashy lightning bolts and a mane like a lion, he thought he was king of the world. Of course, he pretty much was, but he didn't have to be so high-and-mighty about it, sitting on Olympus with the other Olympians and doing whatever it was they did up there. Hades imagined them boasting about their exploits of turning themselves into animals and meddling (to put it lightly) in the lives of humans. (And they called *him* evil.) Sure, he had partaken in his own acts of skullduggery. Hades had tricked the goddess Persephone into being his wife, but she only spent one third of the year helping to rule the Underworld, and the rest of the time she was with the other Olympians or off in other lands, using other names and incarnations. She was the Goddess of Spring in some lands, and Nestis, Queen of the Dead, in others. She was rarely in the Underworld, and after a time, when she was there, she spent the hours in her own part of the kingdom. He hardly knew she was there. For all he knew, she wasn't there at all.

The fact was, Hades had become very bitter and lonely, and he had changed. He had done things he was not proud of, out of desperation and anger, so he shouldn't have been surprised his family saw him differently now, distrusted him, and didn't want his company. Frankly, he didn't even want his own company; he hated who he had become down in the Underworld.

From the instant he took the throne he was reviled and feared by his family, not to mention almost everyone in the many realms. He didn't understand it. Sure, he had become the ruler of the dead, but he didn't feel that meant he had to change who he was. He felt like the same Hades, but without knowing how, he had become the Unseen God, an outcast, with only the dead, his minions, and his dog for company. And he hated it. His life had now been that way for more years than he could recollect, counted only by his increasing bitterness and deep, penetrating loneliness.

As the years passed, he felt himself growing more vengeful and bitter, becoming the god his family treated him as. He was obsessed with filling his halls with *guests*, and seeing to it that none of them escaped.

Nothing made Hades angrier than some poor soul trying to escape his realm. If *he* was forced to reside there, then so would they be. This was when he went mad and tricked the goddess Persephone into being his bride. Together they held elaborate dinner parties for the dead, which became a nightly affair for Hades, even when Persephone would no longer attend them.

Hades would meet his honored guests as they disembarked from the ferry across the river Styx, ushering them through his great fortress and into his splendid dining hall, where he sealed their fates to linger in the realm of the dead for eternity. But all of this felt hollow; these poor doomed souls were there only at his command, which made him feel even lonelier. The last place they wanted to be was in the Underworld, surrounded by despair. They didn't want to be his guests. They wanted to be with their families, with their loved ones, laughing and enjoying the sun shining on their faces, and Hades understood that all too well, because he felt the same. So one night, rather than hold a feast for the dead, he invited his family to dinner, being sure to note on the invitation that he would have his minions obtain the food for the banquet from outside the Underworld. He wanted them to know this wasn't one of his tricks. This was his way of extending an olive branch. He wanted to change. He wanted to be himself again, and he thought the best place to start was with his family.

He arranged to have one of his favorite halls in the Underworld decked out in preparation. He was excited to have it filled with his family and the sound of laughter. He was eager to show them around his fortress, talk of old times, share stories, and prove to them and himself he was still the same old Hades. And he was eager to talk with his brother Zeus. Perhaps repair the bonds that had been broken so many years before.

He was elated with anticipation as he sat at his long black marble dining table, which was carved to look like a great serpent that twisted its way through the room. The inlaid marcasite gleamed as Hades waited for his guests to arrive. He made sure everything was perfect and that his minions, Pain and Panic, put out his finest black china: the set that had a stunning painting of his profile in the center of the plates and were trimmed in gold, matching the skull chalices that would soon be filled with honey wine, and his favorite, pomegranate wine. He made special arrangements for the honey wine to be brought in from Olympus for his family, along with food from their lands that wouldn't render them eternal guests in his kingdom.

The dining chairs were one of his favorite features of the room. They were fashioned to look like dead trees, their leafless branches adorned with the spirits of crows that cawed to one another in harmony by the glow of blue flames in the massive fireplace.

A supernatural blue light also emanated from the eye sockets of the countless skulls that composed the walls of this chamber, laid like stone or bricks, making for a macabre dinner setting. He had done what he could to create a space he loved in the kingdom he despised. And this room was one of his little sanctuaries. Hades truly loved this room and wanted his family to love it, too, and he couldn't wait for them to arrive.

He sat in his dining room, his hand dangling off

the side of his massive throne carved from black marble and edged in gold. He was scratching one of his dog's heads when he felt one of its other heads lick his hand.

"Thank you, Cerberus, but gross," he said, flinging the slobber off his hand and then petting his dog's third head, which looked neglected. "Where are all my guests, Cerberus?" he asked, getting up to pull a braided velvet rope hanging alongside the fireplace. A cacophonous bell rang out through the Underworld.

"Pain! Panic! Get in here!"

The devils scrambled into the great dining hall, slipping on dog drool and sliding across the shining black onyx floor before crashing into Hades's throne. They sat there peering up at him with terrified looks on their faces.

Hades had no idea how he had gotten saddled with these children of Ares and Aphrodite. When the idea to have them serve him in the Underworld was brought to him, he thought it was rather unusual; however, Pain and Panic were renowned for being formidable on the battlefield, so he thought why not have them in reserve should their services be needed.

But as far as he had witnessed, they only proved formidable at annoying him.

"Yes, Your Majesty?" Panic was living up to his name, but not in the way Hades had imagined. He did not cause panic in others but was often panicked himself, especially when speaking to Hades. He was a timid, sickly looking creature, and he was all points. Pointed horns; tiny, pointed wings; a long, pointed nose; and large, round, yellow eyes that were always filled with fear. He shuddered as he waited for Hades to speak, shaking so much that Hades placed his hand on the creature's head to stop him from vibrating.

"Did you deliver the invitations, as I demanded?" Hades leaned down and looked Panic straight in the eyes.

"Yes, sire, we did," said Pain, causing Hades to look in Pain's direction and narrow his eyes in disbelief. Pain was a round little devil, also with tiny wings, and horns considerably smaller than Panic's. And he looked just as frightened as his cohort. The only one to whom he caused pain was Hades. They both looked as though they were bracing themselves for an outburst of anger, which they saw coming. Hades's blue flaming hair was turning red, and the brighter red it became, the more the little devils shook with fear.

"Then where, may I ask, *are all of my guests?*" Hades's head was now burning bright red. A color that reflected his mood. A color that told his minions they were about to be thrown into the river Styx, if they didn't answer in a way that pleased their king.

"Well, sire, you see, everyone on Olympus is getting ready for the birth of Zeus's child; they say he will be born within a fortnight. Oh, and sire, Zeus asked us to give you this." Panic's hand was shaking as he handed Hades the invitation for the upcoming birth's celebration. When Hades opened the envelope, an opalescent winged horse crafted from paper flew out and circled around his head. Hades snapped his fingers, causing the invitation to catch fire, its glittering ashes raining down on him.

"Blah, blah, bah, *Zeus's baby*! That's all everyone is talking about. Even Charon was blathering on and on about the little brat the other night when he ferried me across the river. I asked him, 'Do you bore the dead with this nonsense? For all I know they're still alive when they board your damnable ferry, and your stories bore them to *death*! This is the Underworld, man— what do we care of the goings-on in Olympus?'" He then lowered his voice and leaned down to whisper so there would be no chance of anyone other than Pain or Panic hearing him, even though no one else was in the room. "So tell me, what did they say when you brought them the invitations? What's it like up there? Are they just sitting around drinking honey wine, laughing and floating on clouds all day?"

"Well, sire . . ."

But Hades didn't give Panic a chance to reply. He already knew the answer, and he was incensed. He exploded into flames that emanated from his entire body. He was filled with rage and envy. "It's not fair! I don't get to float on anything!" Hades clenched his fists, his head an inferno, causing all the blue flames in the room to burn red.

"That's not true, Your Majesty, you can float on your rivers of blood!" said Pain, taking Panic by the hand and trying to inch away.

"Silence! Leave me, now!" Hades's outburst made the little devils scatter out of the room. His dog looked at him with sad eyes and curled up next to the fireplace as Hades paced his great hall. He realized his family had never intended to come to his party, and he supposed he shouldn't have expected them at all. If he wanted to see them, he would have to go to Olympus. He hated visiting there these days. Everyone was so golden and filled with light, just sitting around being superior and godlike.

"Nothing has been the same since I became the Unseen God, banished down here while everyone up there is glowing and ethereal, laughing and looking down on me. And I mean *literally* looking down on me. The people used to love me when I was the Giver of Wealth, but now? I'm just a demon who had to trick a goddess to marry him, whose family hates him, and whose only friends are two imbeciles and a three-headed dog. No offense, Cerberus. I hate who I've become. I don't even recognize myself anymore." He glanced at himself in a mirror hanging on the wall, the back of his hand theatrically pressed to his forehead.

"Am I so terrible? Is the Underworld not good enough for them? Too gloomy? Not sparkly enough? Not enough harps?" Hades paced around the room as he continued to rant. "We have cool stuff down here, don't we? We have ferry rides, rivers of blood, skulls, three-headed dogs!" Flames burst from his hands as he gesticulated wildly, then slammed them over and over again on his dining table, making the china rattle and waking one of Cerberus's heads, which had been snoozing with a puddle of drool collecting under its chin. Hades sighed.

"Who am I kidding; it's miserable down here. And I'm a monster. Well, if they won't come down to see me, then perhaps I should pay them a visit once their precious little brat is born."

And without warning, and taking Hades completely by surprise, three women appeared in his hall. At first Hades thought they were dinner guests late for the party, arriving after all, and he felt foolish for being so upset. But when he looked at them, he realized they were not gods but witches. Witches who, he sensed, were almost as powerful as gods. Witches who could be goddesses, if the cosmos aligned just right.

The three witches just stood there, frozen and bewildered, each of them looking exactly like the other, all of them beautiful in a peculiar way. Their eyes were large and bulbous, and their lips were made to look small and heart-shaped with deep red lip paint. Their cheeks were adorned with pink circles, almost like harlequin face paint, and their ringlets were black like the feathers of a crow. It all looked striking against their ghastly pale skin, and Hades immediately liked these witches. But what he liked most was the power he sensed within them.

At last, someone else to talk to.

"Aren't you a delightfully freakish trio! Welcome to the Underworld, my honored guests. You are just in time for the feast I have prepared for you." He played it off like they hadn't taken him completely by surprise. But the witches said nothing. They just looked at him, their heads tilted to one side, trying to take his measure.

"What is it with witches, anyway? Why are there always three of you, is it a rule or something?" He knew the answers to his questions, of course, but Hades loved the opportunity to have someone besides his dog and minions to talk with. And he liked the sound of his own voice. He wondered what could be wrong with these witches, with their stark white faces and too-big eyes, just staring at him and not speaking.

"I know, I know, it's not every day you get the chance to meet the Lord of Darkness. I'm sure you're a little tongue-tied. But please, sit down, I have been expecting you." The fact was, he hadn't been expecting them, and he was keenly interested to hear how they had found their way into his kingdom. But nevertheless, he motioned to the dining table for them to sit down as he walked over to the velvet rope and pulled it again. He would get his answers over dinner.

"Pain, Panic! Bring in the feast! And don't bring that slop you prepared for my ungrateful family! Bring Underworld food, and plenty of pomegranate wine! And clean up that puddle," he added, eyeing Cerberus. "Excuse the mess, dear ladies. You know how it is with three-headed dogs. Three times the drool." He paused for them to laugh. But the witches didn't move from their spot. This was maddening. He finally had potentially interesting company and they weren't talking to him.

"Nothing? Come now, I demand you speak and take your places at the table. Let us celebrate your arrival!" he said with a wave of his hand, causing the flames in the skulls to burn blue to match his hair.

The witch in the middle spoke first. "We know . . ."

And then the second one took over. "You were not . . ."

And, finally, the third witch chimed in. "Expecting us."

Then they all spoke as one: "Unless the King of the Underworld now takes orders from the Fairy Godmother."

"I assure you, dear ladies, I do not take orders from anyone, let alone this Fairy Godmother, who-ever she is!" he said, pulling out a chair so one of the witches might take her seat. But they just stood there, looking at him with their big eyes that grew rounder the longer they stared at him. Perhaps they were sizing him up, or maybe they were devising their escape. There was no way of knowing what was going on in their devious little minds; their power was so great that they had closed their thoughts off to him completely. *These witches are strong. Never mind. I'll let them keep their thoughts to themselves. For now,* he thought as he motioned for them to sit down. But the witches just sputtered fragmented sentences at him, which drove him mad.

"The Fairy Godmother . . ."

"She's a wretched . . ."

"Horrible creature."

"Yes, yes. Why don't you tell me all about her over dinner. But first, a little adjustment." He waved his hand, causing all the witches to jump. It was the first real indication they were capable of movement since their arrival.

"That should do the trick. I cannot abide by the way identical witches speak. It's *so* distracting and, quite frankly, annoying. No offense," he said with a flourish of his hands and a big smile.

The witches just looked at him with their large

eyes, staring at him with blank expressions and their hands at their throats, as if they were choking and unable to speak. Hades rolled his eyes.

"I see you have a flair for the dramatic. I think we're going to get along just fine. You should be able to speak intelligibly now. Go ahead, *try.*" He was finding this quite amusing. He decided he was going to enjoy the company of these witches, or if not, then he'd have some fun tormenting them.

He stood there waiting to see what would happen as he stroked the feathers of one of the ghost-ravens sitting on the back of the chair he'd pulled out for Lucinda. "And in case you have any ideas, you should know your magic doesn't work here. NOW SIT DOWN AND ENJOY THE SPLENDOR OF THE UNDERWORLD!" he said, his head burning with red flames.

"We're sorry, Lord of Darkness, but we don't belong here. We are in the wrong place," said the witch in the middle. The witches were dressed identically. All of them in red velvet trimmed in black lace. They looked as if they had been attending a ball right before they arrived, and he was still wondering how they had ended up in his dining hall.

"That's what everyone says when they come down here. But, eventually, this is where they all end up!" he said while grinning theatrically and doing jazz hands. The Odd Sisters flinched and jumped back in terror, making him laugh. "I'm personally not a fan of the Underworld, either, but I have a feeling it will be a lot more fun with you three here. I didn't catch your names."

"I am Lucinda, and these are my sisters, Ruby and Martha," she said, motioning to her sisters who were standing on either side of her.

Then Hades realized there was something familiar about these witches, something he hadn't gleaned when they first arrived. "You're from the Many Kingdoms; you *don't* belong here. I can smell death on you, but you're not dead, are you? You're descendants of the witches of the Dead Woods. You're the Queens of the Dead!" Hades couldn't fathom how this had happened. Of course, he knew who the Queens of the Dead were, and they knew who he was; all keepers of the dead knew each other. But how were the queens of the Dead Woods in his realm now, so unceremoniously? It was unheard of. He would never venture into their kingdom without an invitation. Not intentionally, at any rate. It was bad form. There had to be a good reason they were there under those circumstances, and he was eager to hear it.

"We are not the queens; we are the oracles of our land, the writers of fates. And we would be grateful if you could return us to the Many Kingdoms," said Lucinda, looking rather taken aback to be speaking independently from her sisters.

"Don't worry, you'll get used to speaking intelligibly," he said with a sly, cheeky grin. The Odd Sisters grimaced in silence. "Interesting," he said, continuing to pet the ghost-raven on the back of the chair he was still waiting for Lucinda to take. "Interesting indeed. Clearly, you're telling the truth."

"Then take us home, demon!" spat Lucinda.

Hades laughed. "Look here, witches, I am in charge! This is *my kingdom*! So if I say sit down and enjoy a delicious meal with me, that doesn't mean act like petulant children. It means SIT DOWN AND HAVE A DELICIOUS MEAL WITH ME!" He waved his hands, causing two other chairs to be pulled out right next to the one he had already pulled out for Lucinda. Then he snapped his fingers, making the Odd Sisters glide over to those seats and sit down at the table. They looked like puppets on invisible strings, helpless and angry.

"I will take you home, if you promise to be good little witches and eat all your din-din," he said. "By the gods, I just realized who you remind me of. You look like Baby Jane!" He couldn't stop laughing. "You know that movie *What Ever Happened to Baby Jane?*"

The Odd Sisters just looked at him.

"Nothing? Really? Whatever. Look, if you want me to take you home after dinner, then you will have to do something for me," he said, his elbow on the table and his chin resting in the palm of his hand.

He was grinning at them, and he could feel it was making them ill at ease. But who did these witches think they were, coming to his realm, not laughing at his jokes, and demanding they be taken home? Of course he would want something in return! He was the king of the Underworld. Hadn't they ever heard of making a deal with the devil? He knew in general witches could be rather unhinged—take his Fates, for example; they spoke in riddles and drove him mad with their half-truths, predictions, and constant flaunting of their powers. At least these witches were more tolerable, and a lot more powerful, even if they didn't know it yet.

"And what would you like, *Your Majesty*? What can we do for you?" asked Lucinda, folding her hands like a perfect little schoolgirl, making Hades chuckle under his breath at the unnaturalness of her posture.

"I haven't decided yet. But once I do, you will be the first to know. We shall seal the deal in blood after dinner," he said as Pain and Panic brought in their feast and poured the wine. "But first, let's make a toast! To new allies!" He raised his glass.

"To new allies," said Lucinda, forcing a smile and raising her glass. Ruby and Martha raised their glasses as well but didn't speak. He guessed they were too afraid to speak, so he let it pass.

"Now tell me, how in blazes did you end up in my domain?" he asked, shooing Pain and Panic away after they finished placing all the serving platters on the table.

"The Fairy Godmother. She was angry with us for trying to help someone, a woman she found unworthy," said Lucinda. She seemed to be the only one of the sisters who felt comfortable speaking in intelligible sentences, as if the other two had no experience with it at all. And the more closely he probed these witches, the more it became clear to him why, but he kept that to himself.

"I see. And why did this woman need your help?" he asked between sips of wine.

"She had been tricked into a loveless marriage by a man who abused and debased her, and we gave her the means to be rid of him for good."

"Aw. Aren't you little Furies. And let me guess, this Fairy Godmother didn't approve? I think someone might need to teach this Fairy Godmother creature a lesson and set her wings on fire! She can't just pop witches in and out of my kingdom without so much as an introduction! Who does she think she is? I might

pay her a visit!" he said, snapping his fingers and causing the flames in the room to blaze more brightly.

This sent the Odd Sisters into peals of laughter
and put them instantly at ease.

"I'd love to see that! You're the last person she'd
want visiting the Fairylands," said Lucinda.

Hades liked these witches, and he was happy to
have laughter in his dining hall at last. After dinner
he moved their little party out to his balcony, which
looked out majestically onto the dark waters of the
river Styx, while they drank more pomegranate wine
from skull chalices. Hades was enjoying the company of these witches and loved hearing about their
exploits. They talked endlessly about their little sister,
whom they loved more than anything in this or any
other world, and how they had tried to help a queen in
their lands named Grimhilde by trapping her abusive
father in a mirror and making him her servant, but
the queen went mad and now was trapped within that
same mirror, which was in the possession of a young
woman they despised named Snow White. Hades
wanted to hear more of their stories, but it was almost

time to send the witches back to their own lands. As much as he loved their company and wished they could stay, he did say he would take them home after dinner—but perhaps he could tempt them to stay a little longer.

It was worth a try. "I suppose I can't talk you into dessert. What's your favorite?" But before they could answer, he had gleaned it from Martha's mind. Her thoughts weren't so masterfully veiled as her sisters'. "Cake? That's your favorite? Then cake we shall have!" said Hades, snapping his fingers and making a cake appear.

"I guess it wouldn't hurt to stay a little longer," said Ruby, accepting the slice of cake from Hades while Lucinda shot daggers at her.

"Don't be such a witch in a ditch, Lucinda. Have some cake!" said Hades, and Lucinda acquiesced after seeing how much her sister was enjoying it. It seemed to Hades the Odd Sisters forgot they were eager to get back to the Many Kingdoms as they munched cake and told him stories about their various adventures, until at last Lucinda, Ruby, and Martha finished the entire cake, put down their forks, and stood up from the table.

"Are you sure you can't stay awhile longer? You don't want to miss watching the dead ushered in on the ferry, it's a deliciously macabre sight," Hades said, but he knew it was time to send them home. He saw it in their hearts.

"We have to get back to our little sister. She is going to be worried about us."

Hades could see they were truly anxious about their little sister, and knew he couldn't delay them any longer. "I suppose this is where we say our goodbyes, then," he said, waving his hand to create a flaming blue vortex. It was a window into another world. The witches' world. The Many Kingdoms. They could see the Odd Sisters' house surrounded by rosebushes on the other side of the portal; it had a roof shaped like a witch's cap, round windows, and a lone apple tree. It looked like a delightful little dwelling, one he hoped to visit soon. "I am going to miss the sound of your voices in my dining hall. You really know how to liven the place up!" he said, waiting for them to laugh. "Anyway, you're much more fun than the sourpuss, know-it-all Fates," He was surprised he was a little sad to see them go. But a deal was a deal. He said he would send them home, and that's what he was going to do.

"Thank you, Lord of the Dead, for everything. We will not forget this," said Lucinda, looking longingly at her house through the vortex.

Hades could sense she was looking for this little sister they were so eager to get back to, and it made him curious to meet her.

"Yes, yes! Please come by anytime you wish for a spot of tea! We will never turn you away if you bring another one of those delicious cakes!" said Ruby. She and Martha both seemed more comfortable now with their new way of speaking. Though he could tell they both still seemed nervous about something.

"Goodbye, our great and exalted king. Please don't hesitate to let us know if there is anything we can do to return the favor," said Martha, flinching when Lucinda stomped on her foot with a pointed boot and glared.

"Oh, Lucinda, you tricky little witch, do you think

I forgot about our blood oath? You thought you could get away without honoring your promise to me?"

Lucinda didn't answer. She didn't have to. Hades could read it on her face and hear it in her mind. These witches might be powerful, but they were not quite as powerful as gods. Lucinda had, in fact, thought he had forgotten. No matter. He probably would have tried to do the same thing given the chance, if he were in their situation.

Hades said, "You must realize that by dining with me, I could make you stay in the Underworld, as my eternal guests. We have no need for a blood oath."

"Then why even mention the oath?" asked Lucinda

"Because I was curious to see if you have a sinister turn of mind, and it seems you do. We have a lot in common, my little pettifoggers. But let's make something clear: I may find you dingbats amusing, but that doesn't mean I won't hold you to your promise. I can and will bring you back to the Underworld for good if you refuse to honor your deal with me.

"Now, off with you," he said, waving goodbye to his new friends. "I'll be seeing you again. Soon."

CHAPTER V

FROM THE BOOK OF FAIRY TALES

The Many Kingdoms

It had been a fortnight since Hades sent the Odd Sisters back to the Many Kingdoms, and in that time Zeus's son Hercules was born. Hades didn't even know why he had bothered to go to the ridiculous and exceedingly tedious brat celebration. He was met with nothing but sideways glances from his estranged wife and awkward silences from the rest of the Olympians. This event was a spectacle for the ages. The Olympians were dressed in their usual finery, shining gold, and fawning over that stupid brute of a baby. Hades knew he was going to grow up to be just like Zeus.

Everyone had gone silent when Hades arrived, and didn't even bother to hide their disappointment that he was there, except for Zeus, who pretended all was well between them. His fakery was insulting, condescending, and belittling. Zeus made a big show of Hades's arrival and piled on the feigned platitudes, not to mention offhand insults and, naturally, jokes at Hades's expense. Everyone laughed, of course. Not that Zeus was particularly funny, but his Olympian sycophantic fools laughed at all of his jokes, even if they were always too on the nose.

It was exhausting, dealing with his brother. Hades wished he hadn't accepted the invitation, and wanted to leave the moment he got there. He didn't have the desire or energy to partake in false pretenses anymore. He was done pretending and trying to hide his bitterness. Things had not been good between Hades and Zeus since the day they stood in the ruins of the ten-year war and divvied up the kingdoms. Hades didn't know why he was even trying; Zeus and the other gods had been treating him like a monster from the moment he took his throne, and now he had become that monster. So after a few quippy remarks, a major dose of snark, and jokes that were far funnier than his brother's, Hades decided he'd better make a quick exit. He was done. No more dinner invitations. No more trying to make amends. No more visits to Olympus until he could take the throne! As he made his way to leave through the gates of Olympus, Zeus followed him for a private chat, brother to brother. (We'll get to that conversation in good time.) But when Hades returned to the Underworld that day, fending off the dead as he floated in his boat down the river Styx, he knew what he had to do. He had a plan. A plan to destroy Zeus.

A different trio of witches was waiting for him when he returned to his fortress in the Underworld— those know-it-all Fates. They assured him he would be successful, his plan would work, and they were certain he would overthrow Zeus. At least they were almost sure. There was always a hitch when it came to know-it-alls.

Hades couldn't abide the Fates' company, but he was encouraged by their foretelling nevertheless, even if it meant suffering their long-winded ramblings and dreadful poetry.

> *In eighteen years precisely,*
> *The planets will align ever so nicely,*
> *The time to act will be at hand.*
> *Unleash the Titans, your monstrous band,*
> *Then the once-proud Zeus will finally fall,*
> *And you, Hades, will rule all.*
> *A word of caution to this tale,*
> *Should Hercules fight, you will fail.*

Okay, sure. It only took him ten years to fight, defeat, and imprison the Titans, but he *could* unleash them if it meant overthrowing Zeus's stupid baby and the rest of the Olympians.

But how to get Hercules out of the way? That might be a bit trickier, since his stupid baby was stronger than one of Zeus's lightning bolts. If only there was a way to turn Hercules into a squealing, helpless, *human* newborn, and therefore much easier to kill. Or at least easier for his minions to kill. Hades saw no reason to sully his hands with the trifling brat. So he created an elixir that would turn Hercules human, stripping away all his powers so Pain and Panic could kill him. Easy peasy.

But it wasn't enough. Hades needed this to work. He needed a guarantee he would be able to defeat his brother. He needed more help, powerful, magical help, and he was going to find it in the Many Kingdoms.

First stop, the Odd Sisters. It was time to call in his favor. After telling Pain and Panic it was up to them to hold down the fortress for a few hours (that was all the time he originally intended to stay, but you know how it is with witches: things always take more time than you expect), he stepped into his massive fireplace, caused the flames within to erupt, and within seconds he found himself in the Many Kingdoms standing in front of the Odd Sisters' home. It was a crooked little house with stained-glass windows and a witch's-cap roof that sat at the top of a cliff. It was surrounded by a rose garden, and in the back, there was a lone apple tree that felt as if it held a special meaning. Around the garden was a white picket fence with a bell at the gate to alert those within if someone was coming. He saw a tortoiseshell cat sitting in one of the windows and looking at him with large yellow eyes. Something about her seemed familiar, but she jumped out of sight when the bell on the gate rang.

When he knocked on the door, he was surprised by who answered. It was a beguiling blond he knew from his own lands, the goddess Circe. She was the daughter of a Titan and a great sorceress known for her abilities to transform her enemies and those who offended her into animals. He certainly didn't expect to find a goddess in the Many Kingdoms, and at the Odd Sisters' house, of all places.

"Circe! What are you doing here?" he asked, but before he knew it, she had grabbed him by his robes, pulled him into the house, and snapped all the curtains closed with a wave of her hand.

"What are *you* doing here, Hades? Did the Fates send you?" She looked panicked.

"In a way they did, but they didn't tell me you were here. I am here on my own business. I repeat, why are *you* here?"

"Many years ago, the Odd Sisters' wish found its way into my heart. They prayed for a little witch sister, and I granted their wish. I bound myself to them in blood, and we are now kin. I am them, and they are me. We are one," said Circe, eyeing Hades. He knew she didn't trust him, just like most of the other gods and goddesses.

"You're not really known for granting wishes. What's the catch? What do they owe you?" asked Hades, scanning the room.

"There's no catch, Hades. They're my family now. They don't *owe* me anything. And just because I'm not known for granting wishes doesn't mean I can't. We're gods; we can do whatever we want."

"Whatever. You don't have to tell me if you don't want to. So, do they know who you really are, or do they think they conjured a little sister from the ether?" asked Hades, looking around for the cat he had spied in the window and wondering where the Odd Sisters were. He was only half listening to Circe. He knew there had to be more to her relationship with the Odd Sisters. Circe was renowned for powerful magic and vengeful ways. Then it clicked. She liked them because they reminded her of herself.

"They think I am truly their sister. And so I am. I looked into their hearts, Hades, and what I saw there hurt me to my very core. I wanted to help them. So we are sisters now, in spirit and in blood. And as far as they know, this is how it's always been," said Circe.

"These witches are far more powerful and interesting than even I gave them credit for," he said, feeling pleased with himself that he had thought to bind the Odd Sisters with their promise to him. If the goddess Circe found these witches worthy enough to become their true sister, then they were truly remarkable. Far greater than he had guessed. They had the blood of a goddess running through their veins; they would be very useful indeed.

"I won't let you hurt them, Hades, or allow you to bring them into your schemes, even if it may be fated," she said with a great sigh. She walked over to the kitchen table and picked up a book. It was a great tome bound in leather with gold letters that read THE BOOK OF FAIRY TALES. "I haven't figured out how this book works. It's clearly written by the Odd Sisters, or at least by their magic, but there are stories here that date to back before they were born, stories written by their mothers and grandmothers, I believe. But those stories are sometimes hard to find. I'll sometimes see glimpses of them, never to find them again," said Circe, looking at the clock sitting on the fireplace mantel.

Hades didn't understand what this had to do with him. He didn't need to be getting caught up in whatever Circe had going with the Odd Sisters. Yes, these witches amused him, but he was here to collect on their deal, not learn their history.

"Look, blondie, I don't have time for this. What does any of this have to do with me?"

"It has everything to do with you. That's what I'm saying. Your fate is connected to the fate of these witches, and to mine, and we need to figure out how. But I don't have time to talk about this right now. I'm meant to be in the Fairylands," she said, conjuring herself into a young girl with blond hair. "The Dark Fairy Maleficent is taking her fairy exams today, and the Odd Sisters and I will be in attendance."

"And why the disguise? Is this how you appear to the Odd Sisters?"

"No. It's because the Fairy Godmother won't object to my being part of the exam if she thinks I'm a little girl," she said, making her way to the door, clearly eager to leave.

"I know I'm going to regret asking this, but who is Maleficent, and why in blazes would she have to take a fairy exam if she is already a fairy?"

Circe sighed. "She's taking her exams to become a wish-granting fairy, and she could use our support. The other fairies don't like her because she's different from them. Again, I don't have time to explain. It's all in the book; read it and we'll talk when I get back," she said. But before she took her leave, she turned around, and even though she was in the shape of a little girl, all golden, cherubic, and filled with light, she had the most serious look on her face. If he were anyone other than the Lord of Darkness, he might have been intimidated.

"I will not let you hurt my sisters, Hades. And I will do everything in my power to protect them.

Everything," she said. Then she walked out the door.

Hades rolled his eyes. Was he doomed to forever be surrounded by witches who offered nothing but endless threats and prophecies? First the Fates, and now the great witch goddess Circe? One of the most powerful sorceresses in the pantheon? Something had to be done about her. He needed to think. Maybe there was something in reading this Book of Fairy Tales. Maybe the answer to how the Odd Sisters could help seize power from Zeus was in those pages. So he decided to make himself a cup of tea, sit down at the Odd Sisters' kitchen table near the large round window, and read this book. The Many Kingdoms were more interesting than Hades had expected.

While he read, it became clear the Odd Sisters had a fondness for, and felt protective toward, women who were wronged in some way. And even if their methods were often misguided, Hades saw a pattern emerging from the pages: the Odd Sisters were trying to help these women. As he read more of the Book of Fairy Tales, he started to fall in love with this land: its stories, its creatures, and, most of all, its witches.

He saw many similarities between this realm and his own. The Cyclopean Giants and Tree Lords were like the Titans from his world; the Odd Sisters were like the Fates, or perhaps even the Furies; and the fairies, when he thought about it, were like his family on Olympus—snooty and superior, always passing judgment and getting angry and uncomfortable with anyone who wasn't like them. And the longer he sat in the Odd Sisters' kitchen, the more at home he felt in the Many Kingdoms. He sat there for hours, reading all the stories—stories from the past and the future, some of them heartbreaking, and some that were inspiring. He loved the sketches of the different kingdoms and their varied architecture; he loved researching the family trees and reading about all the inhabitants in the Many Kingdoms and their stories, which reminded him of the sagas from his own world. It didn't hurt him as deeply anymore that his family didn't make him welcome on Olympus, and most importantly he no longer felt so lonely. And then something came over him, a feeling he did not expect—he felt more like himself than he had in many years. He felt the inklings of who he was before he came to rule the Underworld.

The more he read, the more he grew to like these witches. Their stories delighted Hades to no end, and they broke his heart. He was sure, as Circe suspected, that some of the stories were being kept from the Odd Sisters. So he read their stories voraciously, stories about the Odd Sisters' lives and their past that they didn't even know about, looking for ways in which they could help him. He suddenly realized how mortals could fall in love with their favorite characters in the books they read, how they felt they knew them, and how they came alive in their imaginations. But he was reading about real people, real witches, and he couldn't wait until they returned.

The more he learned about the Odd Sisters, the closer he felt to them. They had a connection, shared similar histories—and it was clear they shared a fate. He started to daydream about living in the Many Kingdoms and popping over to visit the Odd Sisters anytime he pleased, and decided in that moment he needed a place of his own in this land. He needed a place to stay while he figured out how he was going to overthrow his brother. And he should probably be nearby to make sure the Odd Sisters didn't find a way to betray him in some way, which, he gleaned from the Book of Fairy Tales, they had a habit of doing every time they "helped" someone. Yes, this was the perfect way to get what he wanted. He didn't need to think of that horrible conversation he had with Zeus before he left for the Many Kingdoms, the one that led him there to ask the Odd Sisters for their help. He didn't want to think of the odious Fates and their warnings about Hercules, or his empty throne in the Underworld. He had found a place where he felt at home, and he would stay there until he figured out how the Odd Sisters could help him with his goals. So right there on the spot, he dreamed it into being, a foreboding castle, which he named the Forbidden Mountain. It would be a place to relax and get away from the pressure of being the ruler of the Underworld. The castle would be perched on a remote and craggy cliff, and covered in glowing green moss, with stone ravens and gargoyles, and in the deepest bowels of the castle the flames of his realm would burn before a great throne made of stone—a throne he would surely rarely sit upon, with the whole of the Many Kingdoms to explore. The flames would be a direct portal between the Underworld and the Many Kingdoms, so Pain and Panic could come get him should anything go amiss while he was away. Yes, this was the perfect plan, he thought.

It was a castle fit for the King of All Evil, a keeper of the dead, but the fact was he wasn't feeling particularly evil now, and he preferred the idea of spending time with the living.

"You can't hide from your fate forever, Hades."

It was the Fates, decrepit and foreboding. They looked out of place in the Odd Sisters' kitchen, with the daylight pouring in through the stained-glass windows. Before he met the Odd Sisters he had thought most oracle witches were like these haggish creatures. He hated the reminder that he wasn't of this world.

"What do you three know-it-alls want?"

"The question is, what do *you* want, Hades?"

"I thought you knew everything! Besides, I already told you, I want to dethrone my brother and take over Olympus!" said Hades, his head now burning red with anger.

"And you want to stay here," said the Fates, narrowing their eyes at him. He knew they weren't wrong. He did want to stay. "Yet your presence in the Many Kingdoms will cause a chain of events that will bring destruction to both our world and this one. Did you know that when they were babes, your Odd Sisters were spirited away from the Dead Woods for fear of their formidable power, fear of the destruction their madness would cause, and through that act, they have been set on that very path of ruin and madness?"

"I think I might have read something about that in this book," he said dismissively, and continued. "But what has that to do with me? It sounds like the Odd Sisters and these lands are doomed, with or without me. I'm here to collect a favor, simple as that."

"Then why did you build yourself a castle? There is no escaping fate, Hades. Not for the Odd Sisters, and not for you. These witches are like you—they will stop at nothing to achieve their goals, no matter who they destroy in the process. This was their fate from the moment their mother sent them from the Dead Woods. The Odd Sisters will rip their souls asunder, all in the name of their dearest Circe. They will think they are helping, yet they will do nothing but destroy, and you will do the same if you choose to stay here and not take your place where you belong."

"Then I will demand their mother take them back and set the course right, one ruler of the dead to another. We'll avoid all the madness and destruction. Problem solved. Geez, am I the only critical thinker around here?"

"If you've read the Book of Fairy Tales, then you know their mother has passed beyond the veil and there is no reasoning with her. The Odd Sisters have only just learned of their connection to the Dead Woods, because *you* brought it to their attention when they appeared in the Underworld. When they learn their entire story, they will make the sky red with blood, and the stone angels will weep. This is their fate; do not interfere. Every story in the Book of Fairy Tales is threaded together like a spider's web: cut one string, and you will destroy more than one life. These sisters are the makers of fates in this land, but they will become the Furies. They are not to be meddled with."

"Not exactly the answer I was hoping for." The Fates' words gave Hades a terrible feeling of foreboding. "What aren't you saying?" he asked, an uncustomary chill moving throughout his body.

"We see now that you are too intricately woven into the Book of Fairy Tales, and we cannot untangle you. We cannot cut that thread, and we fear for the future of your kingdom and for all of our fates. The only thing we can do now is help you."

"Oh, so now you want to help me? I thought there was no way of escaping my fate without destroying the cosmos. Do you need a moment to get your story straight, or are we going to stick with this narrative? Because honestly, I can't keep up!" Hades was getting angry and impatient, and the last thing he wanted was for the Odd Sisters to walk in and find these hags in their house. It was one thing for him to be there; they owed him a favor. It was another having a know-it-all town hall meeting in their kitchen.

"There is one way, but it's dangerous. You would need to split your string of fate. It will take witches even more powerful than us to achieve this, but it seems you have the means to make use of the very witches who may be able to help you. If they can find the spell they need in the books of their mothers, you will be able to reside here *and* in your own realm."

"Isn't that your thing, cutting strings? Why can't you just do it?" asked Hades, feeling even more impatient.

"We cut strings, not split them. There's a big difference."

"Fine. So there would be two of me? Like a copy? Running around looking, acting, and talking like me? Will he be funny and devilishly handsome? What am I saying? Of course he will."

"Not a copy. He will be you, and you will be him. One and the same."

"And will he—I—agree to this?"

"He will. And you will both get what you want.

Together, along with the Titans, you will be able to defeat your brother. The other Hades will take over Olympus, and you will be free to stay here, if you wish."

"What makes you think I want to stay here once I win?"

But the Fates disappeared. Their only answer was their mocking laughter, which still lingered in the Odd Sisters' kitchen after they left.

Leave it to those know-it-alls to tell him what he wanted! But he did think their plan was delicious. And he did love to live deliciously. Two of him was better than one, he thought, and he decided that was the favor he was going to ask of the Odd Sisters. He would ask them to split his fate string. The Fates had said they would need the right spell, but that shouldn't be a problem. Nothing would stand in their way . . . except Circe. He knew in his cold black heart that Circe was the only person who might interfere with his plans. She had warned him she wouldn't allow him to bring the Odd Sisters into any of his schemes. He had to do something about Circe.

CHAPTER VI

FROM THE BOOK OF FAIRY TALES

A Secret and a Promise

Hades was still in the Odd Sisters' house waiting rather impatiently for them and Circe to return from the Fairylands. "Where are those devilish women?" he asked no one but himself as he poked around, looking at their books, peeking into their cabinets, and riffling through their drawers. He spied an interesting collection of teacups, all of them different from one another, and it made him laugh. He had read in the Book of Fairy Tales and the Odd Sisters' journals what could be done with teacups and thought how much he liked the way these devious witches' minds worked. He also spied an assortment of treasures, just tucked away behind the jars of tea and mismatched cups, and wondered who the poor souls were who had originally been the owners of those items, again laughing, because he had a feeling those items would likely be cursed in the future—that was, if they hadn't been already. He made a mental note to himself to go back through the Book of Fairy Tales and keep an eye out for anyone who was wearing those items. It was interesting getting to know the Odd Sisters in this way, reading about them and having their house all to himself so he could snoop around, alone and undisturbed.

At least he thought he was alone, until the beautiful cat he had seen in the window came slinking into the room through a little door that led in from the back garden. She had little bits of leaves, flower petals, and twigs in her fur and spiderwebs stuck on her whiskers, like she had been rummaging around doing catlike things, even though she didn't seem very catlike to Hades. And he wondered if she wasn't someone who had offended the witch goddess Circe and had been turned into a cat.

"Hello, Hades," she said, blinking her yellow eyes and adjusting her two front paws, one right after the other, before she started cleaning her face with one paw. It was Pflanze, the Odd Sisters' cat. Hades had read about her and found her to be an amusing and formidable character. He had a sense she was no ordinary cat—if she was a cat at all. He could feel the great power within her, but this creature seemed to keep her secrets to herself, and, according to the Book of Fairy Tales, it was clear she was fiercely protective of her witches. She reminded him of a goddess he hadn't seen in a very long time, and he wondered silently who this cat really was.

"Hello, Pflanze. I'm waiting for your witches. Circe said it was okay."

"You didn't bring cake," the cat said, blinking her eyes at him again.

He snapped his fingers and conjured a cake, making it appear on the kitchen table. It was round and covered in dark chocolate frosting, and had a raspberry filling. "Hopefully this will do!" he said, smirking at Pflanze.

A Secret and a Promise

"You seem like the sort of god who likes secrets. If I tell you one, will you make me a promise?"

This took Hades by surprise. He was almost sure Pflanze had heard his thoughts. He was intrigued. He had a feeling she was going to tell him who she really was. It was too irresistible to pass up.

"That depends on the promise *and* the secret. Is it juicy?" Hades had a feeling it was, or he wouldn't be bothering with a talking cat. For all he knew all the animals in this kingdom talked, but he did know there was something very different about this creature. He leaned in closely as Pflanze whispered the secret into his ear.

"Oh, I knew it! That *is* a good one!" he said. "Do your witches know?"

"They don't, but Circe does, and I'd prefer to keep it that way until the proper time."

"That's fair. So, what's this promise? I suppose you want to whisper it into my ear as well?" he asked, leaning in again, and the moment he heard it, he decided the bargain was worth it, with one small addendum. "It's a deal. But I need one more thing

99

from you before we seal it. Tell me why the Odd Sisters and Circe are at this fairy exam, or whatever she called it. Why is this Dark Fairy so important to them?"

"The Odd Sisters are aligning the cosmos to ensure Maleficent transforms into a dragon and destroys the Fairylands, as it is foretold in the Book of Fairy Tales."

"Ah. And I suppose it doesn't hurt to have the great witch goddess Circe there to help them. I see they didn't need my help getting revenge on the Fairy Godmother! Good for them. So how do I find the Fairylands?"

"The Fairy Godmother won't welcome you in her lands," said the cat, her eyes flashing in the sunlight coming through the stained-glass windows.

"That's not a problem," he said, stretching out his arms and turning himself into a crow, with a long, sharp beak and striking black feathers tinged with blue. "She won't know it's me."

"Take to the sky and feel for the witches' vibrations. Follow them until you find the Odd Sisters," Pflanze said,

adjusting her white paws. They reminded Hades of fat little marshmallows.

"Good kitty." With a wave of his wing he conjured a saucer of milk for her before opening the front door with his magic. He hopped (as birds do) over the threshold, spread his wings, and took flight, soaring into the clouds, letting out a loud caw of thanks. He could see Pflanze below getting smaller as he ascended above the clouds, and he wondered how long it would take before he had to fulfill his promise to Pflanze. If he had any doubts before about the Odd Sisters' ability to split his fate string, they were now completely obliterated. These witches had the power to direct the cosmos. He was going to call in his favor, and together they were going to destroy his brother Zeus.

Hades flew higher and higher, soaring in and out of clouds. The view of the Many Kingdoms was astounding. He felt for the witches' vibrations, but something distracted him—the vibrations of another witch, a witch he didn't know. Her vibrations of grief, loathing, and despair were so strong that Hades couldn't help but go toward them, and when he finally found their source, a feeling of deep sadness overcame him. He was in what was left of a dark forest, now blackened with ash and soot. The only thing alive was a single apple tree, the green leaves and red apples showing vividly within the black landscape. It reminded him of the apple tree in the Odd Sisters' back garden, and he realized its significance.

He landed on one of its branches, still in his bird form, wondering who could have caused this. Surely it was the witch he had felt through the ether, and he sensed she was no longer of this world, yet somehow she hadn't gone beyond the veil, either. And then he saw it: the old king and queen's castle, abandoned and overgrown, fallen into disrepair. The Black Forest was situated between the old kingdom and a small hamlet where the dwarves lived and worked, and he remembered who was responsible for the blight in the forest. He had read about Queen Grimhilde in the Book of Fairy Tales. Hades felt each time he read one of the stories he learned something new about the Odd Sisters. He wondered if a witch who was queen of this land was capable of such destruction, then what would the Odd Sisters do when they learned of their true origins? Would it be as the Fates described? Would the sky rain blood, and would the stone angels weep?

And then the Fates appeared, as if he'd summoned them with his thoughts. They stood on the black earth, ghostly and frightening. Their mouths moved, but words did not come forth, and their images flickered in and out of view before they became solid and he could hear their warnings.

"Hades, heed our words, there is a reason you were drawn to this dead place. This forest is imbued with a hate so consuming it destroyed the land and its wielder. The reason you feel a connection to the Odd Sisters is because they, too, are fated to dwell with the dead. It is their fate as well as yours. Though you may be choosing your own path, you will still walk among the dead."

Hades's crow feathers were covered in a cold mist, and a chill went through him as he watched the

Fates disappear. He took off from the lone apple tree and circled above the bleak forest, wondering if it would ever recover as he searched for the Odd Sisters' vibrations. But he was distracted—something else was calling to him. It wasn't the Odd Sisters. It felt familiar and yet entirely new.

Then he saw it, the Forbidden Mountain, and it was just as remarkable seeing it with his own eyes as it had been when he'd imagined it into being. He flew around his new fortress, looking at the stones covered with green moss, at the raven and crow statues, and the dark beauty of his new palace captivated him. He flew through a window in one of the high towers and down a dark tunnel. He decided it would be easier to navigate in his true form, so he transformed into himself again and followed the vibrations that were calling to him. He felt the same pull he had felt when he was drawn to the Black Forest, and he felt he had to follow it, even though he was losing time and needed to get to the Fairylands. The tunnel was pitch-black, so he created a flame in his hand and ventured down the long passage that twisted and turned for miles, until he realized the stonework in this part of the cavern was different from the stone in the castle he'd created; it was covered in gray moss rather than green, and he realized the catacombs under his own castle were somehow connected to those of another. And just as he was starting to feel that this passageway was leading nowhere, it opened up into an immense and opulent hall with tall marble pillars and elaborate arched alcoves that contained statues. The stone floor was shrouded in a heavy swirling mist that clung to his robes and chilled him like the mists in the woods.

In the center of the room was a dead tree, and next to it a massive and stately statue of the formidable and horrendously cruel witch Manea. He read her name on the plaque at the foot of her statue and recalled what he'd learned of her treachery in the Book of Fairy Tales. And at once he knew where he was. He was beneath the Dead Woods, in the dead queen's death chamber. He had made a terrible mistake in allowing himself to be drawn there. The statues of the former Queens of the Dead looked at him with hollow eyes, reproaching him for entering their domain, so he bowed to them in reverence. It was not customary for the keepers of the dead to enter one another's kingdoms without being invited, without pomp and circumstance, but he was lord of the Underworld, after all; who were these witches to stand against him? It was as if the Queens of the Dead heard his thoughts, because the statues began to move, and the one of Manea in the center near the dead tree let out a horrific scream that woke the other statues from their slumber. Blood seeped from the statue of Manea's eyes while her screams grew louder and shriller, and the walls began to tremble, causing cavernous cracks that birthed thousands of skeletons, which poured into the room and piled at his feet.

He looked down at the skulls and bones lying at his feet and smirked. "Now I see where your daughters get their flair for the dramatic!" he said with a smile he hoped would charm the Wraith Queens.

"The dead are always welcome here, Lord of the Underworld. Your coming was foretold. Choose your next step carefully, Unseen One; you hold the fates of many of us in your hands."

"I hold the past Queens of the Dead in the same esteem as my own Fates, and they've uttered the same warning. Can your daughters not take their place as queens here?"

"All of my daughters have betrayed me or are fated to do so in the future. I will not reach out my hand to help them ascend the throne, nor will I ever welcome them beyond the veil."

"Well, maybe if you just told them who they are and let them take their rightful places, you wouldn't have this self-fulfilling prophecy nonsense on your hands! Ever think of that?" Hades's head burst into red flames. Even he was surprised by his anger, but the Wraith Queen Manea reminded him of his brother, and the hate he was now feeling for both of them was becoming all consuming.

"You stand on the bones of the queens who came before my daughters. You stand in the halls of my mothers, and those who attended them. My daughters do not belong here, and neither do you. We are connected in death, Lord of the Underworld, but we are not friends."

Hades felt a sadness within him for the Odd

Sisters. Their family had abandoned them, just as his family had abandoned him. Their mother cast them from their rightful place, just as his brother banished him to the Underworld. He felt a deepening kinship with these strange women and decided he would do whatever it took to help them.

"Then I shall take my leave of you, great queen, and let you rest in peace." He bowed, just as he would expect her to do if she were visiting his realm. "And I promise never to enter the Dead Woods uninvited again."

"See that you never do, Lord of Darkness," said the miserable queen as she and the other statues slowly took their places of rest once more. It was all so disturbing, knowing these were the Odd Sisters' true family, and he wondered how much of these Wraith Queens' attributes resided within Lucinda, Ruby, and Martha.

Hades shook his head as he left the chamber, knowing full well he was more powerful than the Wraith Queens, but he didn't want to waste his time or energy by starting a war with the Queens of the Dead—he needed to save that for Zeus.

As he made his way back through the catacombs, he let his mind drift to the last time he saw his brother. It was at Hercules's birth celebration. He hadn't wanted to think of it; he kept pushing it from his mind, even though it was the very thing that had brought him to the Many Kingdoms to ask the Odd Sisters for help. He couldn't help but think of it now.

He remembered standing at the gates of Mount Olympus before he made his way to the party. He was struck by how different he felt while on Olympus. It was so open, so full of light, and surrounded by stunning nimbus clouds. He just stood there breathing deeply and enjoying the space around him. He felt free when he was on Olympus. In the Underworld he felt confined and anxious. The sulfurous air choked him and made the walls close in on him. He wanted to look up and see clouds, golden and pink, and to breathe the fresh air, and he wanted someone to talk to who wasn't dead.

Hades took his time that day making his way to the highest point of Olympus, where he knew he would find his brother and the other Olympians celebrating the birth of Hercules. He loved walking the winding path that took him up and around the beautiful realm. When he reached the top, he walked into the party, which was already in full swing. All the gods and goddesses were in attendance. Zeus greeted him, grinning with everything but his eyes. That's how he was: he would flash that smile while scanning Hades with a suspicious look in his eye. And it all went as Hades expected. Zeus was annoying, and Hades was snide. Zeus made jokes at Hades's expense, and everyone laughed. So Hades left with a renewed hatred for his brother. But before he could make his way back to the Underworld, he heard Zeus calling after him. He had followed Hades out so they could talk alone.

"What is this all about, Hades? Inviting us to dinner?" asked Zeus, no longer needing to put on a show for the other Olympians, no more pretense of joviality or friendly sibling jibing.

"I don't know, Zeus. Maybe it was an olive branch, or perhaps I had a temporary loss of my senses," said Hades, not even wanting to look at his brother. He was done. He wanted to leave, but Zeus kept talking.

"Everyone knows food consumed in the Underworld renders the visitor an occupant," said Zeus. "You don't honestly expect us to believe you weren't trying to trick us, the same way you did with Persephone?"

"You're right, Zeus, I was trying to trick you!" Hades was being sarcastic. "Oooo! The bogeyman Hades was trying to trap the great and powerful Zeus in the Underworld. As if you didn't make the laws or have the power to change them at will! We both know you just didn't want to come."

"No, I didn't. Look at you! You've changed. You're hideous. No wonder you had to trick someone into being your wife! You've become a monster, Hades. You're evil, bitter, and cruel."

"And it's been by your design! Watch your back, brother. Next time you hear from me, it won't be an invitation to dinner. It will be a declaration of war!"

Hades sighed, trying to banish the memory of that conversation from his mind. Trying to root himself back in the Many Kingdoms. He was angry with himself for being foolish enough to think that after all this time he could invite his brother over for dinner and they'd have a little chat and work things out. It was madness to think they'd ever be friends again. If they ever had been.

He didn't care for either of his brothers, really, but Poseidon was another story, one that he found in Ursula's story in the Book of Fairy Tales—although Poseidon was called Triton there—a story that didn't surprise Hades one bit. Both of his brothers valued beauty over everything else. (Well, almost everything else. The thing they both valued most was power.) It had become clear to Hades that Zeus didn't want him on Olympus, offending everyone with his hideous visage. Zeus would rather exile his own brother to rot with the dead, to become putrid and foul. His brothers no longer loved or valued him; they saw him as a monster. When he allowed himself to admit that, it hurt him deeply. He felt more certain than ever that his decision to take over Olympus and cast his brother Zeus into the Underworld was the right path. The only way forward now was war—and he would do whatever it took to win it.

CHAPTER VII

FROM THE BOOK OF FAIRY TALES

The Forbidden Mountain

Hades had originally intended to go to the Fairylands, but it became clear that his travels that day would only take him to the dead places of the Many Kingdoms, and he had had enough of dead places for the time being. Instead, he traveled back through the catacombs that seemed to connect the Dead Woods and the lower dungeons to his own fortress, and he contemplated what to do next. He made himself comfortable in what would become his favorite room in the Forbidden Mountain, laughing at himself because even though he had made a point of trying to make it different from his palace in the

Underworld, he now realized there were similarities.

He sat there, taking in the room, loving the way he felt there. Rather than skulls, the dominating features of his new fortress were ravens and crows. He adorned it with numerous statues of his favorite avian creatures, and their eyes blazed with green fire to match the green moss and vines that permeated the stone fortress. In his new dining hall, he had a large, round, black marble table, and at its center was a sculpture of a dead tree where the spirits of crows rested and cawed to one another. Occasionally they fluttered down to visit with the other wraith crows, which resided on the chairs that he now realized looked just like the ones in his dining hall in the Underworld. Throughout the fortress, green flames hung in the air like fireflies, dancing to the crow songs, which captivated Hades, giving him tiny moments of peace. He contemplated his life so far, realizing it hadn't been a good one, but he was always thankful for the glimmering instances that brought him peace and even happiness, even if just for a moment. This was one of those moments.

Hades sat at his dining table, petting one of the crow spirits, deciding how he was going to set his plans into motion. He would send a message to the Odd Sisters, inviting them to his new castle after the fairy exams were over. He conjured a roll of parchment, a quill, a pot of ink, a length of sealing wax, and his official seal, and quickly scribbled a note to the Odd Sisters letting them know he was there and would like them to attend upon him at their earliest convenience. And by earliest convenience, he meant *now*. He folded the note, melted a blob of wax onto the folded parchment, and placed his seal, which of course showed a dignified image of his profile. Then he handed it to one of the wraith ravens. "Take this to the Odd Sisters. You will find them in the Fairylands," he said, and he watched the ghostly raven fly out of the window. He envied the raven's ability to travel so freely. Even in his bird form, Hades wasn't truly free. Perhaps once the Odd Sisters split his fate string and the other Hades had taken up residence in the Underworld and their plan to overthrow Zeus was in place, he would explore more of the Many Kingdoms and see all the magical places he'd learned of while reading the Book of Fairy Tales. But now was not that time. He needed to set things into motion. First he had to deal with Circe. It was clear she was wildly protective of the Odd Sisters and wouldn't allow them to do such dangerous magic. Hades decided the best thing to do was send Circe to a place for safekeeping and bind her to keep her from ever returning to the Many Kingdoms. But how to do it without the Odd Sisters knowing? How to do it so they wouldn't journey to find her and bring her home again?

As he sat there considering his options, he was becoming impatient waiting for his raven to return with the Sisters' reply, so he conjured a small swirling vortex that allowed him to see where the Odd Sisters were. He found himself looking upon the Fairylands. Everything was in chaos. Fairies were screaming and running in every direction as fire rained down from above. A great dragon was casting green flames at them, and it was engulfing the lands. The Odd Sisters scrambled, trying to run toward the fire. They were crying Circe's name over and over, afraid she was caught in the flames. Hades knew the goddess Circe couldn't succumb to such a death—she was too powerful—but he remembered Circe had enchanted the Odd Sisters into thinking she was just their sister and not a goddess who had answered their prayers. This was the perfect opportunity to get rid of Circe, and the Odd Sisters would think she was dead, killed by the dragon's flames. It was the only way. He had to do it if he was going to achieve his goals; besides, the Fates had said it was Circe who would send them down their path of destruction. Perhaps this act wasn't so selfish after all; nevertheless, he knew if the Odd Sisters were in his place, they would do the same.

He searched for Circe with the use of his vortex and found her, still in the guise of a little girl. She was trying to release some crows from a cage when he reached into the vortex and yanked her through the portal, leaving the cage behind.

"What in blazes are you doing?" asked Circe, now transforming herself back into her real form. "The Dark Fairy is attacking the Fairylands. I am needed there." She flung her hand in an attempt to leave, but she was surprised to see her magic was no longer working. "You've bound my magic! I wanted to trust you, Hades, I really did, but there is no way I will let you drag my sisters into this war you have with Zeus. I will not let you endanger them or anyone else in the Many Kingdoms."

"I know. That is why you have to leave. Goodbye, Circe," he said, snapping his fingers and making her disappear.

With that obstacle out of the way, he was one step closer to defeating Zeus.

CHAPTER VIII

FROM THE BOOK OF FAIRY TALES

A New Circe

It had been weeks since the Odd Sisters lost their sister Circe. The fairies were hard at work restoring the land that had been destroyed by Maleficent, and no one knew where she had gone. The Odd Sisters were distraught, exhausted by their grief over the loss of their sister and their worry over Maleficent. Hades hadn't expected their grief to be so prolonged, and he was doing everything he could to help lift their spirits so they'd be strong enough to help him. And when he let himself admit it, he hated seeing them suffer so terribly.

He had taken to just letting himself into the Odd

Sisters' house without knocking. Today, he found that the kitchen table was filled with the numerous cakes he had brought over on his previous visits. He sat the new cake on the table, after making room amongst the others, and looked around to see where the Odd Sisters might be. They were not in their sitting room, where he usually found them, poring over their journals and spell books or calling to Circe and Maleficent in one of their magic mirrors, to no avail. Instead, they were in Circe's old bedroom, all of them lying side by side, squished in her bed, just staring at the ceiling. Staring into nothingness.

"Okay, ladies. Time to get up, I've brought you some cake," Hades said, clapping loudly and smiling widely as he hovered over them. The Odd Sisters remained catatonic, their eyes unmoving. He wondered if they even knew he was there. That was, until Ruby murmured, "No more cake."

"What's this? An Odd Sister who doesn't want cake? This must be serious." Hades was doing his best to be jovial. To lighten the mood. He knew his usual fiery tactics wouldn't work if he wanted these witches to regain their strength so they could perform the spell he needed. Besides, he had already tried threats, and they hadn't worked. He reminded them they were still considered his honored guests in the Underworld, and that at any moment he could imprison them there. But they didn't care. They said they'd rather be in the Underworld than live in the Many Kingdoms without their sister. So Hades had to come up with yet another plan.

"This is deathly serious," said Lucinda, who was sandwiched between her sisters, looking Hades dead in the eye.

"Come now, get out of bed, the three of you. I know you're grieving, but we mustn't let ourselves waste away. I got you a delicious hazelnut cake. *Your favorite!*"

"That's not our favorite! And we're never getting out of bed again. Our sister is dead, and we've lost Maleficent," said Ruby.

Hades knew the Odd Sisters were tired of him coming over every day to check on them and speed along their recovery, but he was losing time. If he couldn't get them to agree to help him soon, he would have to go back to his own realm and fight Zeus without their help. And as much as he didn't want to admit it, he did care for these witches.

"What if I told you there was a way to create a new Circe, and I can help you?"

The Odd Sisters sat bolt upright, like toy vampires popping out of their coffins. They looked ghastly and malnourished and even paler than usual. Their hair was matted, their makeup smeared, and they were still wearing the same dresses they'd worn the day they thought Circe had died.

"Holy Nosferatu!" he said, startled at their appearance. "All right, Miss Havishams, the first thing we need to do is get you out of those dresses." He reached out his hand to help them out of bed, one by one. They looked at him as they often did when he said things they didn't understand. He waved his hand, putting them in new dresses of black velvet with silver star embroidery, black-and-white-striped stockings, and black pointed boots. "And maybe we should do something about these rats' nests," he said, looking at their tangled ringlets caked with frosting. "I almost feel like a Fairy Godfather!" he said as he magicked their hair into perfect ringlets again, dressing them with jaunty feathered hats fashioned with crows sitting in nests of black netting. The sisters looked at him, dumbfounded. "You know, because I'm giving you a makeover!" he said, his arms stretched out like a vaudevillian.

"Don't start doing your pizzazz hands. We're not in the mood," said Ruby.

"They're called jazz hands, and I wasn't going to. Look, I'm really trying here. I'm pulling out all the stops. Hair, makeup, dresses, shoes, just like the Fairy Godmother." And that was all it took—the mere mention of her name sent the Odd Sisters into a fit of anger so fraught with malice they were storming around the room and plotting their revenge. Hades understood. When he wasn't procuring the Odd Sisters cakes, trying to revive their spirits, or checking in with Pain and Panic to make sure they hadn't managed to destroy the Underworld, he read about the events that led to Maleficent destroying the Fairylands. And they were right. It had pretty much been the Fairy Godmother's fault. If she hadn't been so cruel to Maleficent, treating her like an outcast, deciding she was evil because of the color of her skin and that she . . . gods forbid . . . had horns, Maleficent would have likely never become so angry, triggering her transformation, even with the help of the Odd Sisters aligning the cosmos. The Odd Sisters set the scene, they made it possible, but it was Maleficent's heartbreak and anger that caused the transformation. And it was the Fairy Godmother who caused that heartbreak.

"I will skin her alive!"

"Then I will boil her in oil!"

"Not before I rip her wings from her back!"

"*What have you done?*" Pflanze was staring at him from the Odd Sisters' vanity. She was annoyed. "*Hades, I finally got them settled down right before you arrived.*" Her tail was swishing violently, and her eyes were narrowed and angry.

"I had to do something! It's better than the

alternative. They were catatonic!" Hades said, giving her a scratch behind the ear.

"*Is it?*" she said, jumping off the vanity and slinking toward the door. "*Well, now you have to deal with them. I need a break.*" She exited the room with a swish of her tail. Hades decided it was better that it was now just the four of them. He wasn't sure what Pflanze would think of his plan.

"Ladies, now look at what you've done—you've sent Pflanze away. Don't you want to listen to my plan? You will have time enough for your revenge after you've created a new Circe," he said, hoping this would be the way to get them inspired. He had read in the Book of Fairy Tales that the witches of the Dead Woods had great powers, necromantic and otherwise, and numerous spell books that held their secrets. And he learned from his crows that there were young, inexperienced witches out there now, trying to take their places as the queens of that land, but they were struggling and would be grateful to meet other witches who could help them. So he decided it would be best to send the Odd Sisters there in the guise of offering their help so they could go through those books to find the spell they would need to create another Circe and split his string of fate. Of course, it would be easier to just go there and get the spell books himself, but he did promise the Wraith Queens he wouldn't enter the Dead Woods again, and if it was within his power to do so, he always tried to be a demon of his word.

"A new Circe?"

"Yes, a new Circe, wouldn't that be grand? Just like the other one. All I ask in return is that you cast a spell for me."

"What kind of spell?"

"It's not a big deal, really. I just need you to split my string of fate in half so there will be two of me."

They stared at him. "And how do we do that? We don't possess that sort of magic. We don't even know the spell."

"But you have the power! The Fates told me so. Now you just need the spell. You have ties to the witches of the Dead Woods, so you won't have trouble entering the woods, and you're just as entitled to the magic of those lands as the young witches who reside there now. Visit Gothel and her sisters in the Dead Woods, don't tell them who you are, and while you're there, look in their mother's spell books. There has to be something there that shows you how to split fate strings and how to create a new Circe."

"And we're supposed to just walk into the Dead Woods and say, 'Hello, let me see your mother's spell books'? Gothel isn't going to think that's strange?"

"I think she and her sisters would be happy to meet other witches. Happy for some help. From what I understand, they could use some. I hear Primrose and Hazel are unwell. You can offer to help them look for a cure in their vast library. It would give you an excuse to poke around and find the spells we need."

The Odd Sisters looked intrigued, and Hades could see their thoughts racing. "And if we do this for you, split your string, we will be even?"

"We shall see," he said, seeing his plan was coming together at last.

"But we can't go off to the Dead Woods to help

other witches while Maleficent is still lost. What if she attacks another kingdom and someone tries to kill her?" said Ruby.

"Leave Maleficent to me. The crows are keeping an eye on her for me. I will find her and make sure she is safe. You go to the Dead Woods and find the spells we need, and I will lend you my powers to help you in any way I can. And, listen, this is important: when you get to the Dead Woods, try not to act so Odd Sistery."

"What do you mean?"

"You know exactly what I mean. These young witches have been through enough without you talking all crazy and doing your weird Odd Sisters stuff. Just be their friends. Wouldn't it be nice to have some friends?"

CHAPTER IX

FROM THE BOOK OF FAIRY TALES

The Sleeping Dragon

Hades had his hands full looking after Maleficent while the Odd Sisters were away, so he was pleased when they finally made their way back to him from the Dead Woods. He had been spending more time in the Forbidden Mountain and decided to do some decorating to bide his time while he waited for their return. He created a lower dungeon beneath the throne room by way of a narrow set of stairs that led down to a cavernous room with a monstrously large fireplace with a blazing fire. The fireplace was flanked by two enormous dragon statues, and before it was the sleeping Maleficent in her dragon form.

Hades had put her under a sleeping enchantment so she could rest and recover after her ordeal. Since Maleficent's arrival, Hades's crow and raven spirits often flew down to the dungeon to check on her. They felt protective of her now, since it was them Hades had sent out in search of her. On one of their searches they had found Opal, Maleficent's crow, and brought her back to the Forbidden Mountain so she could tell Hades her story. The moment she told him where he could find Maleficent, he magically transported the dragon into his dungeon, and that is where she would stay until she had time to become herself again. Time to let go of enough of her heartbreak, terror, and rage.

When the Odd Sisters finally arrived, Hades was sitting in his throne room, petting Opal, who was perched on the armrest. It was the Odd Sisters' first visit to his castle, and he was happy to be in the company of his witches once more.

"Welcome to the Forbidden Mountain, witches! I thought you would never return! How do you like my new digs?" asked Hades, smiling at the Odd Sisters.

"Digs, have you been digging? Why not just use your magic?" asked Lucinda, making Hades laugh.

"I'm so happy you dingbats are back. So did you find the spells we need?" he asked, letting Opal hop onto his shoulder.

"We're happy to see you too, but we promised Gothel we would return to the Dead Woods soon and try to help her with her sisters, Primrose and Hazel. They are dangerously ill and fading fast," said Lucinda. The Odd Sisters seemed more focused to Hades, much more than they had been before they went to the Dead Woods. He had hoped giving them a purpose would help, and it seemed it had.

"We're so disappointed we couldn't find anything in their spell books to help poor Primrose and Hazel, or to bring Circe back," said Martha.

"If I didn't know better, I would say you're fond of these witches. You should go back as soon as possible. I am sure the answers are there, to both that and how to split my string," said Hades.

"Oh, we found the spell for the string," said Lucinda, giving Hades a devilish grin.

"Way to bury the lede!" he said, startling Opal with his bombastic voice. "So tell me, what did you learn?"

"We found an interesting spell, one that can split a witch into three, and we think with some modifications we can use it to create two of you."

Hades wondered if the Odd Sisters understood the implications of the spell they had just described, but they just kept chatting away, and he decided they hadn't made the connection. His witches were smart—they tended to be singularly focused when they put their minds to something—and yet they would often completely succumb to being distracted from their purpose.

"Tell us, did you find Maleficent? Is she safe?" asked Martha.

"Oh, I found her," he said.

"Is she okay? Where was she?" asked Ruby.

"She was on the verge of attacking Morningstar Kingdom. Opal here found me in time to save her, but I put Maleficent under a sleeping spell before she could do any more damage. She's resting safely."

"We should visit her!"

"Don't get distracted from your purpose, my witches. Let the Dark Fairy rest and recover for now. She is full of grief over what she did in the Fairylands," he said.

"The Fairy Godmother deserved what she got!"

"I agree. But let's get back to this spell to split my fate string. How long do you think it will take to perfect it?"

"Not long. By the next full moon. Then the time will be right," said Lucinda, who seemed to have a gleam in her eye.

"So only a few days from now? And you can have it ready by then? Good. I have plans of my own, and there needs to be two of me to achieve them," he said. Just then, Pflanze came into the chamber. She had been stopping by to check on the Dark Fairy since she learned she was sleeping in the lower chamber.

"Pflanze! Welcome back. I hope you're well."

The tortoiseshell cat walked into the throne room as if she were the queen of the place, making Hades chuckle, considering who she really was.

"I'm well enough, Hades. And I see my witches are in better spirits. I came to see if all was well with them, and to check on the Dark Fairy. Where is she?"

"Where she's been every time you've visited her—in the lower dungeon, keeping warm by the fire. She is still sleeping," said Hades, loving that he knew a secret about Pflanze that the Odd Sisters did not know.

"May I go down and check on her? I won't disturb her," she said, narrowing her eyes at him, no doubt hearing his thoughts and reminding him with her reproachful looks to keep his mouth shut.

"Of course. You are, as always, my most honored guest, here or anywhere I may reside," he said with a sly wink. "Remember, it's the narrow stairway on the left. Please don't go lurking down the wrong passageways; you might find yourself among the dead."

"Thank you for the warning." Pflanze stretched before taking her leave and heading down to the lower dungeon to see the sleeping dragon.

Hades saw the looks of bewilderment on the Odd Sisters' faces. But he knew it wasn't about Pflanze.

"There are two portals down there, one to my realm and one to a chamber below the Dead Woods. I know, I know, I should have told you about the one to the Dead Woods, but I wanted you to become friends with the witches there. I didn't want you just skulking in and out like the sneaky little witches you are, finding what you came for and rushing home. You need friends, witch friends, and who better than the witches of the Dead Woods? Someone to think of as family." Something had happened that he didn't expect: he was allowing himself to admit he cared about these witches. He had been telling himself he was simply sending the Odd Sisters to the Dead Woods to get the spell he needed, and while that was true, he also wanted them to discover who they really were without all the chaos, blood, and destruction the Fates had foretold. And before he could truly take it in that he was actually fond of these batty witches, the Odd Sisters surrounded him, hugging him and giving him kisses on his cheeks, with tears in their eyes.

"What is it? What did I say? Get off me!" His cheeks were now covered in red lip prints.

"You like us!" they said, grinning at him wildly.

"Oh, stop it!" he said, trying to wipe the lip-paint marks off his cheeks.

"You might not want to admit it, but you like us!" they all said, laughing and jumping up and down like giddy schoolgirls.

"Oh, off with you! You have a lot of work to do! Spells to perfect. Now get out of here, you dingbats," he said, trying not to let on that their gesture touched him, or that they might have been right

As Hades watched the Odd Sisters skitter out of his chamber, he wondered what he had gotten himself into. Did he truly care for these witches? And would it prove to be a mistake letting them into his cold, black heart? Only time would tell.

CHAPTER X

From the Book of Fairy Tales

String of Fate

On the night of the full moon, Hades met the Odd Sisters at their house. As he stood before their front door in the twilight, he looked at their funny little home and wondered if it was the last time he'd pay them a visit. Though he did have faith in his witches' abilities, this was very advanced magic, and he wanted to be prepared if it didn't work and he was forced to return to the Underworld. He took a deep breath, and just as he was about to snap his fingers to make a cake appear in his hand, Martha called out through one of the windows.

"No need to conjure a cake! We made one for

you!" she said, popping her head back inside just as quickly as she had popped it out.

"Yes, Hades, come inside!" said Ruby, standing in the open doorway. The Odd Sisters had decked themselves and the house out for a splendid celebration. Lucinda, Ruby, and Martha were wearing blue dresses with delicate beadwork flames that appeared to dance in the light. Their hair was pinned in elaborate updos, with long, soft ringlets and blue ribbons that fell over their left shoulders. Glowing blue gems were woven into their hair, along with jaunty blue feathers at the crowns of their heads. Hades hadn't seen such pageantry since he'd visited eighteenth-century France.

"Holy Marie Antoinette, you look fabulous!" he said. "I suddenly feel underdressed." He magicked his robes to match their dresses. "There! Now we're all fabulous! I mean, we're pretty much *always fabulous*, except that one time when you had cake in your hair, but . . . oh, never mind." For the first time, Hades hardly knew what to say. The house was decorated with blue paper chains and garlands of every blue flower imaginable, and the kitchen was filled with delicious-looking cakes, his favorite cookies, ice cream, candies, pots and pots of tea, and everything else he had complained he didn't have in the Underworld. They had created a banquet fit for a god.

"Why do I feel like this is my last meal?" he asked.

"Well, it may be the last meal you have with us. It's near impossible to kill a god, but we are meddling with your fate string, and it's dangerous magic. We're hoping the worst that happens is we're unsuccessful and you will have to go back to the Underworld," said Lucinda, and Hades was glad he had thought to put a spell on the Odd Sisters to make them speak in longer sentences when he first met them. Whenever it wore off he just snapped his fingers and they were delightful conversationalists again.

"And if this does turn out to be our last night together, we want to make sure it is one we will always remember," said Martha.

Hades just stood there, stunned and speechless, the thought of which made him burst into laughter. The Odd Sisters didn't know why he was laughing, but they joined him anyway, all of them laughing, singing, and eating cake until shortly before midnight.

The wooden raven popped its head from the doors of the raven clock on the mantel and cawed, "The witching hour is almost upon us! Caw, caw!" then went back inside.

"Leave it to you to set your clock for right *before* the witching hour!" said Hades.

"That way we will never miss it! What's the sense in the clock cawing at the stroke of midnight when we still have preparations to make before the witching hour?" said Ruby.

Hades didn't answer; he was distracted, looking at the trinkets and framed portraits on the fireplace mantel. There was one of Circe. He was surprised to feel a twinge of guilt for making the Odd Sisters believe she was dead. Well, hopefully they would have a new Circe soon enough. And he had decided that he would do anything he could to help them. It was the least he could do.

"Before we begin, I have something to tell you. Even if the spell works, I will have to go back and forth to my own realm, just for short visits. I won't be gone long," he said, wincing, hoping the Odd Sisters didn't overreact.

"We thought you would be here to help us with the spell to create another Circe if our magic isn't strong enough. Besides, we will miss you." said Lucinda. Hades was fond of all the Odd Sisters, but there was something different about Lucinda. The spark within her was more brilliant than Ruby's or Martha's. They were all exceptional witches, but something about Lucinda burned brighter. And he knew why. He just wondered how long it would be before they learned, and he wanted to be in the Many Kingdoms when they did. He was going to do his best to help them avoid all these doomsday predictions uttered by the Wraith Queens and the dreaded Fates. He had two goals now: defeating his brother, and ensuring the Odd Sisters' happiness.

"If we are able to create another me, then I have to fight by his side. I want us to release the Titans together and defeat our brother. Then he can take Zeus's place on Olympus, and I will be free to stay here and help you. There's time enough to decide what I want to do after that." He was bracing himself for their theatrics, but they were all distracted by a knock on the door. And Hades knew at once who it must be. His head burned red with fire. "YOU INVITED THE KNOW-IT-ALLS?"

"Don't be angry! We need them here!" said Lucinda.

But he ignored her and grabbed a big bowl of candy from the table, then opened the door with a big flourish. "Ah look, it's trick-or-treaters dressed as haggish witches," he said with a wry smile.

The Fates looked comical to him, with their giant eyes and exaggerated features. They were completely out of place in the Many Kingdoms, and even more so standing at the Odd Sisters' front door. This wasn't how he wanted the evening to go, but he was going to make the best of it. He snapped his fingers, and plastic jack-o'-lantern pails appeared in the Fates' hands. It made him laugh to see them standing there like children in grotesque Halloween costumes.

"Happy Halloween! Now get in here quick,

before you scare the locals!!" he said, putting candy into their pails. The Fates seemed taken aback, but the Odd Sisters laughed and laughed, even though he was sure they had no idea what he was talking about.

"It's not Samhain," said the Fate with their one great eye, taking the candy from the pail and sniffing it.

"Yes, I know. That's the point!" Hades said. "No sense of humor, these three." Then, turning to the Odd Sisters, he asked, "What are *they* doing here? Why don't we invite all your witch friends and have a big witchy party? Want me to resurrect your friend Grimhilde? How about Ursula? While we're at it, why not invite Baba Yaga! We'll have to change the banquet to accommodate her unique tastes, but that shouldn't be a problem." Hades was burning red with fire, his eyes bulging and fists clenched.

"Calm down, Hades." Lucinda took Hades by the arm and led him into the kitchen, where they could speak privately.

"Why are you so upset they're here?" she asked him.

"They ruin everything, *everything*! They're always

going on about how my plans will fail," he said, magically morphing his face into the Fate with the eye. "Ooooo! I'm spooky, I'm a know-it-all Fate, blah, blah, blah. It will be a disaster; all will turn to dust. Oh, and by the way, I know everything!" He morphed back to his own face. "It's tedious. Just for once, I'd like to make a plan and not have those hags tell me it will go wrong! I don't trust them."

"But aren't they the witches who have the power to cut Fate strings? And doesn't cutting a Fate string mean death?" Lucinda asked, putting her hand on his arm.

"Yes," he said, his hair now turning from red to blue.

"That is precisely why I wanted them here. I want you alive. This way I can keep an eye on them, make sure they don't get a little too twitchy with those scissors. "

"Ah, you are a tricky little witch, and I love you for it!" he said, surprising both Lucinda and himself, but it was true. "Yeah, I said I love you, so what? Let's not make a big deal out of it and cry or anything," he said, dragging her back into the sitting room with a renewed enthusiasm.

"All right, witches, I'm ready! But the question is, are *you* ready to create another handsome devil? Get it? Handsome devil? No? Okay, whatever. I guess the real question is: do you think the world is ready for two of me?" he asked, putting his hands up and wiggling his fingers with a devilish grin. The Fates just stood perfectly still holding their trick-or-treat pails, looking at Hades, dumbfounded.

"He's just bedazzling. It's a thing he does," said Ruby, looking at the Fates.

"I think you mean pizzazzing! The first time he did it we thought he was trying to put a spell on us!" said Martha, laughing so hard she fell on the floor.

"No, I told you, they're called jazz hands! *This*, my witches, is bedazzling!" said Hades, spinning in a circle, then stopping to reveal that his robe was now completely covered in sparkly blue gems. "And *these* are jazz hands! But I think you're right, pizzazz hands sound more fun!" he said, wiggling his fingers again, making the Odd Sisters laugh so hard now that Ruby was on the floor with Martha. The Fates just stood there with their stupid Halloween pails, staring at them.

"Oh, never mind, you hags are no fun!" he said. "Let's just get on with the spell."

It suddenly became very quiet. A chilly mist enveloped the room, obscuring all the light except a soft glow that illuminated the Fates as they spoke.

"The Witching Hour is almost upon us. It is now time for the splitting ceremony," said the Fate with the long, pointed nose in a voice that grated on Hades's last nerve.

"Yes, yes," said the Fate with the long face and toothless grin. "The time is nigh."

The Fate with one eye and sharp teeth just stood there with her dreaded rusty scissors, snipping them over and over, like she was eager to see everything go wrong and have an excuse to cut Hades's string altogether.

"See! This is what I'm talking about. Everything with them has to be so dramatic!" Hades said, rolling his eyes. "Mists? Really? And stop snipping those scissors! Dear gods, let's get this over with so these hags can get back to boiling the bones of small children or whatever it is they do besides torment me!" He snapped his fingers, making the trick-or-treat pails disappear.

"Hey, we liked those," the Fates said, speaking as one.

"Well, if you're good little witches and I don't die in this ceremony, then maybe you'll get them back!"

Hades and the six witches stood under sprawling oak trees, their branches filled with tiny dancing blue fames that flickered and grew brighter as the witches spoke their incantations from the shadows. Hades was illuminated by a single shard of moonlight streaming through the branches as the witches surrounded him, all of them wearing black hooded cloaks. Their voices were murmurs at first, then grew louder until they rose together in a maddening cacophony.

"Why do I feel like I'm in history's most horrifying production of *Macbeth*?" he said. The witches shushed him as one.

As their voices sang out into the darkness, they

mingled with the breeze, causing the flames in the trees and the moon and stars to shine brighter. Even though it was midnight, the light became so bright the sky grew to be the color of twilight. Hades could feel the cosmos shifting, and suddenly the sky went dark, and the light, instead, filled Hades.

The light from the moon, the stars, and the flames throughout the Many Kingdoms were now all within him. He could feel the stars moving, aligning in a position of power; he felt their light stir within his body and push his fate string out of his chest. Lucinda had warned him that this part would be uncomfortable, warned him that his instinct would be to flee, but he stood very still, resisting the urge to run or put a stop to the whole thing. He kept playing her warnings over and over in his mind: *Everything within you will want to fight against it. Your soul will feel like it's being ripped out of your chest, you will want to resist. Just stand still and trust us. Do you trust me, Hades? Do you trust us?* He did trust the Odd Sisters. Honestly, he didn't know why, there was nothing in their history that would suggest he should, but he did. It was inexplicable, this trust, and this connection he had with them. So he stood completely still, resisting the urge to flee, and to his astonishment he saw it: his fate string emerging from his chest, glowing in the darkness, growing longer and longer until it felt like it was going to rip his heart out with it. At the other end, pulling the string, was Lucinda.

She crooked her finger for the Fate Future to join her and took a knife from her cloak pocket. Future pinched the end of the string between her fingers and held it taut while Lucinda carefully sliced it lengthwise until she reached Hades. The other witches' voices rang out into the darkness, louder and louder, until that and the pain in Hades's chest was all that existed. He felt faint and dangerously close to death, but he held fast to the words the witches chanted over and over.

Make what was one into two,
Bring his double into view.
Grace our realms with more than one,
Untangle this web he has spun.

Bring two Hadeses to us this night,
His brother Zeus he must smite.

The witches recited the lines over and over. Hades felt like he was trapped in an endless loop, taking him deeper and deeper into the darkness, until finally he felt himself enveloped by the vast emptiness of the cosmos. He was fading, dying, and the last thing he saw before he closed his eyes was Lucinda's smile.

CHAPTER XI

THE LIGHTING OF THE DEAD WOODS

Hades paused the Book of Fairy Tales with a dramatic flourish, bringing their party back to the present. They had been listening to Hades's story for hours. It was dark now, and the tables were filled with empty teacups and little plates of cookie crumbs.

"I assume my mothers betrayed you," Circe said. "How did you survive?" Hades understood why she would think the worst of her mothers.

"They didn't betray me, little witch. They created two of me, just as I asked."

Being in the Dead Woods with Circe, Primrose, and Hazel made him miss his friendship with the

Odd Sisters. Hades had grown to think of Lucinda, Ruby, and Martha as family, and he was disappointed when their friendship eventually ended badly. But he had felt a protectiveness toward them, the same protectiveness he was now feeling toward Circe, and he wondered if it was because she embodied the things he loved most about her mothers.

"If the spell worked, then why is Zeus still ruling Olympus?" asked Circe, bringing his mind back to the present. He decided the shortest answer would suffice.

"Because Zeus is a big old baby and has to have everything his way. And I guess it was, you know, *fated*," he said with a flourish of hands.

"We're all just playthings, then, for witches like your dreaded Fates and my mothers? I refuse to accept that," said Circe, and he could see how hurt she was.

"Seriously, Circe, what you, Primrose, and Hazel are doing for the Dead Woods and the Many Kingdoms, what you will do in the future, it's beautiful. It was meant to be. Primrose has seen it in her waking dreams. You are the Circe who was always meant to be queen," he said, smiling at her.

"Wait. Are you saying all of this happened so I would become Queen of the Dead?" She didn't look convinced. But Hades could see the changes her influence had already made; he could see the changes she would make in the future, together with Primrose and Hazel.

"Your mothers started with good intentions. Just like you, they felt everyone deserved someone to protect them, not just the princesses. And do you know why it was so important to them? Because they knew all too well what it was to be alone in the world, to not have someone to protect them, until the day the goddess Circe agreed to be their sister. And I took that from them, left them alone to figure out how to create you. It's not entirely their fault they became corrupted, and they were no longer the witches they once were."

"And we know why that is," said Circe, looking out into the darkness of the Dead Woods.

"They chose to use the best parts of themselves to create you. But don't blame yourself. I'm the one responsible. I am the one who sent the original Circe away. If I had been there to help them as I promised, maybe things would have turned out differently. That's why I felt I owed your mothers one last favor, and agreed to take you from the Place Between. I ruined their lives, Circe. I owed them at least that. My only consolation is that if I hadn't sent the original Circe away, you would have never existed. You would have never become queen, and the Dead Woods would still be a place of terror." Hades noticed Jacob was standing in the doorway waiting quietly until they stopped talking. So he directed his gaze at him and flashed his dagger like smile, even though his heart was hurting to finally admit all of this aloud. He wasn't accustomed to sentimentalities, let alone sharing them with others.

"May we help you, good sir?" Hades asked, smiling at the man. They all turned to look at Jacob. He was wearing a smart black velvet suit and top hat, with a small red rose pinned to his lapel. Hades was pleased with this happy diversion. "Don't you look like the dandy gentleman!" said Hades. "All you're missing is a fancy walking stick." He snapped his fingers, and one appeared in Jacob's hand. It was long and black with a silver crow for a handle and a silver tip at the end.

"Thank you, I am most honored by your generous gift and spirit," said Jacob, spinning it with pride. It was the first time he'd seen Jacob smile since he had arrived in the Dead Woods. This was the sort of man he needed in the Underworld. Hades had been taking mental notes during his time in the Dead Woods and was thinking about the changes he'd like to make when he got home.

"You're like something out of a Dickens novel. Oh wait! You've got to say it! 'You'll be visited by three ghosts.'" Hades was cracking himself up. Of course, Jacob and the witches had no idea what he was talking about, but he didn't care. He loved making himself laugh. He knew no one funnier. "Ah! I know what's missing," Hades said, snapping his fingers again and making a monocle appear on Jacob's face. "Yes! Now you're perfect." Hades couldn't help but smile at this man. He really liked Jacob, and he was happy the man accepted his gifts in the spirit they were intended.

"You look very handsome, Jacob! Every bit the gentleman we know you are," said Hazel, tears in her eyes. "I don't know why we hadn't thought to get you some new things."

"You've been busy, my queen. Don't let your heart be disquieted. I know you love me," Jacob said, and a tear slid down Hazel's cheek.

"Yes, Jacob, wait until Snow sees you next time she visits. She's going to swoon!" said Primrose, lightening the mood. Hades could feel that Jacob took their words sincerely; he knew how much these witches loved him, which was only outmatched by the love he had for them. Hades was quite jealous of Jacob, cheating death as he had and living eternally in the company of such fine witches.

"I'm pleased to see you living so well now, Sir Jacob. You deserve every happiness after what you've suffered, what you've endured. I am envious of the life you have now," said Hades, and he could feel his words touched Jacob so deeply that he didn't know how to respond, so Hades quickly changed the subject. "I'm afraid I am keeping you from the reason you came in here in the first place, Sir Jacob. Please forgive me," said Hades, loving the way Primrose and Hazel were smiling at him.

"Yes, please excuse me, Lord and Ladies of Darkness, but dinner is being served in the dining room, from where you'll have a brilliant view of the lighting of the Dead Woods. If you would please follow me," he said, motioning his skeletal hand as if to usher them out of the room.

"Thank you, Jacob, but I think I'd rather be known as the Lady of Light," said Primrose, her face beaming as her laugh rang out, making everyone else in the room join her.

"I think in time you will all be known as the Ladies of Light," said Hades, escorting the group out of the library and into the dining room.

The dining room was large and rectangular, its walls gray stone like the rest of the oldest part of the mansion. One side of the room had a low wall, so it was open to the elements. This would normally give way to a view of the entire grounds, but it was pitch-black in the Dead Woods now, and the only light in the dining room was coming from the large fireplace in the shape of a massive dragon's head, with a fire blazing within the dragon's mouth. On either side of the dragon's head, Hades noticed oval shapes on the stones that were lighter than the rest of the walls, revealing where portraits used to be— he assumed they were of the previous queens, likely taken down by Hazel and Primrose.

After helping everyone to their seats, Jacob stood near one of the pillars on the side of the room that had a view of the grounds. It was a chilly evening, but the room was warm from the crackling fire that sparked from the dragon's mouth.

"It must be hard for you to live here after everything that hag of a mother did to you," said Hades, making Primrose laugh.

"It feels like many lifetimes ago now, Hades, but thank you for saying so. I think that's why we're determined to bring a new era to the Dead Woods, and to the Many Kingdoms. But how do you know so much about us?" asked Hazel.

"I am a god, Hazel! I know everything. Everything

that's written in the Book of Fairy Tales and more," he said, drifting off into another time, as the ladies of the Dead Woods often did themselves. "Isn't it interesting how family has the power to hurt us so deeply? They can hurt us like no other."

"I think I read a line like that in Grimhilde's story—or maybe it was Ursula's, I can't remember," said Hazel.

"That's my point. Almost all of us have been hurt by our families, but look at us now, making families of our own, with people we choose to love," said Hades, feeling saddened that he had been estranged from his chosen family. He missed the Odd Sisters as they once were; he missed sitting in their kitchen drinking tea and laughing with them and telling jokes they didn't understand.

"Listen to me, I sound like one of those sentimental fools in a made-for-TV movie. I'm afraid I'm giving you quite the wrong impression; I am usually not this sappy." Hades looked at the witches sitting at the table with him, feeling content for the first time since he did the same with the Odd Sisters.

"I think we have the perfect impression of you, Hades," said Primrose. "I'm happy you feel like you can be yourself around us."

As the witches and Hades chatted, Jacob picked up a small silver tinderbox and ignited it, causing the flame to burst brightly in the dim room, getting their attention. He lit the candles that lined the low wall one by one, and when he lit the final candle, the Dead Woods were suddenly infused with light, causing the party to gasp in delight.

Hades got up from his seat and stood near Jacob, looking at the endless sea of candlelight flickering in the darkness. He could see all the faces of the dead illuminated by the candlelight peering at him through the darkness, and was awed by the thousands of souls that resided in these woods. He suddenly had the urge to put his arm around Jacob's shoulders.

"This is one of the most beautiful spectacles I have ever seen. Thank you, Sir Jacob." He was inspired by the Dead Woods. Inspired by Hazel, Primrose, and Circe. They didn't choose to be rulers of this land, and they were nothing like the queens who came before them, but they were making the lands their own and creating something new and unique. They weren't falling into bitterness and despair; they were creating something beautiful.

Hades sat back down at the table as the skeleton servants came into the room, lighting more candles and carrying trays upon trays of desserts. On the long stone table that was draped with a deep red tablecloth were bowls of homemade ice cream with fresh berries, thick, fluffy whipped cream, warm chocolate fudge, shiny red cherries, delicious-looking cakes, bowls of candy, and, of course, multiple pots of tea.

"Oh, look at this! Thank you, Primrose!" he said, grinning. "This is so thoughtful, just like the feast I had with the Odd Sisters." This was just the sort of thing he'd expect of Primrose; she was the most fun witch in the bunch—and the sweetest. He loved them all but especially looked forward to adventures he might have with Primrose in the future. He was surprised he already loved these witches, but something about Primrose made his heart feel happy and light. He liked that he didn't always have to be on with these witches, and so far, they hadn't made him lose his temper, not once. That must have been some sort of record. It was exhausting having to constantly cloak himself in sarcasm. He liked that he could show all the sides of his personality and still feel safe. Just as he had started to do with the Odd Sisters before things went tragically wrong.

"I didn't arrange this feast, and I know it wasn't Hazel, since I can never talk her into having dessert for dinner!" Primrose said, laughing.

Hades wondered if somehow Jacob had overheard the Book of Fairy Tales playing in the library and took it upon himself to make this seemingly little gesture that actually meant so much to Hades.

"It wasn't Jacob," said Circe.

Hades hadn't adequately shielded his thoughts from Circe. *Never mind*, he thought. *I have nothing to hide from these witches.* Hades hadn't expected Circe to warm to him; he was frankly surprised she hadn't lashed out and blamed him for everything she'd been through, blame him for what happened to her mothers.

"If anyone is to blame, it's the previous Queens of

the Dead," said Hazel, also reading his mind. "A pervasive evil has resided in this land since its creation; it was cultivated, celebrated, and became more perverse with each generation, causing a putrefaction of the previous queens' souls. And that foul magic was passed from one generation to the next; that is what caused the Odd Sisters to become what they are. And we refuse to ever let ourselves or the Dead Woods succumb to that ever again. The Odd Sisters are as much victims as we were," said Hazel, her eyelashes glistening with tears, making her gray eyes sparkle in the firelight.

Hades was thankful Circe had Primrose and Hazel. He looked forward to what lay ahead for the Dead Woods with these fine witches as queens, with Primrose shining her light in dark places, her mind to the future, and Hazel helping them to both explore the past and see it clearly, while Circe rooted herself in the present, fighting for what she loved. They were the Fates of this land, the new Odd Sisters, and it sent a shiver through his body, realizing this for the first time. And he felt a bit sad that the Odd Sisters never took their places as queens in the Dead Woods as he'd hoped they would.

At least he could help these witches fulfill their fates, and perhaps change his own in the process.

"All hail the new Queens of the Dead! All hail Queens Circe, Primrose, and Hazel!" Hades said, reaching for his goblet and motioning to the witches to do the same. "Shall we continue listening to the Book of Fairy Tales while we enjoy this scrumptious feast?" Hades conjured the book in his hand and put it on the table to the right of his place setting.

"Why not? I'm ready for some more pizzazz hands!" said Primrose, making everyone at the table laugh again.

"Well then, let's spice things up and have it read in my voice, shall we? I am a much better narrator, anyway," said Hades.

"You can do that?" asked Primrose

"My dear, of course I can. If Cruella De Vil can do it, than why shouldn't I? I am a god, after all; I can do whatever the blazes I want," said Hades. He tapped the book with his long fingers, and the Book of Fairy Tales started to play, reciting the rest of Hades's story in his own voice.

Chapter XII

From the Book of Fairy Tales

A Tale of Two Hades

So there were two of me, and as you could imagine, it was *delightful*. It was twice the fun, twice the devilry, and twice the pizzazz hands. I never tired of letting everyone know how much I enjoyed my own company. After the string-splitting ceremony, the party disbanded; the Fates went back to their realm, and the Odd Sisters returned to the Dead Woods to look for a way to create a new Circe. I told them if they found the spell they needed, I would use my powers as a god to help them.

I brought the other me to the Forbidden Mountain so we could make our plans to overthrow our brother.

The Odd Sisters gifted us with two of their magic mirrors so we could stay in contact with each other when the other me eventually went back to the Underworld—not that we needed them, but I think the Odd Sisters liked feeling as if I owed them a favor, and the fact was I *did* owe them, but not because of the mirrors. I owed them a great debt because I had taken their sister away, allowed them to think she died in a fire, and I just sat there watching them mourn. Of course, mourning wasn't something that usually affected me. I am literally surrounded by death—and I am not in the habit of feeling guilty, but I did. I felt guilty for what I had done, and the other Hades chided me for it mercilessly, and at every opportunity. Honestly, he was a bit of a jerk.

Though the Odd Sisters and the Fates said the other Hades and I would be exactly same, that wasn't quite true. The other me was more like I was before I came to the Many Kingdoms, fueled purely by his hate and bitterness, and honestly, I didn't see a problem with that. We have our reasons for hating our brother, and our life in the Underworld, and if he wanted to hold on to all that and use it for our fight against our brother, then more power to him. We had decided that while he took my place in the Underworld, he'd keep me apprised of everything going on there, and I would lay the groundwork for our attack from the Forbidden Mountain. And even though the Fates had told me I would release the Titans and defeat my brother, the insufferable know-it-alls didn't tell me how I was going to do it. But I was off to a diabolical start. There was just one tiny detail that everyone seemed to overlook. The matter of the Titans. There was no way I was going to be able to waltz up and say, "Oh, hey, remember me, Hades, the guy who helped Zeus defeat you and put you in this stinking pit? Yeah, so, I'm back, and I'm going to release you, but don't attack me, just go after my brother, okay?"

I needed to be sure they would be on my side. So I lied.

Zeus had put five of the Titans we defeated in a vault at the bottom of the ocean. The Mountain King, the Lurker, the Lord of Flame, the Mystic Voice, and Cyclops. They weren't the brightest bulbs in the old pantheon vault, but they were strong. The Mountain King was just as you would imagine: he was a giant two-headed mountain. The Lurker was made of ice and had all these snazzy ice powers, and the Lord of Flame was a behemoth lava monster. The Mystic Voice was a massive tornado creature who could destroy almost anything with his powerful cyclones, and everyone knows what a cyclops looks like—and if you don't, well, let me tell you, you don't want to get into a staring contest with one.

I created a portal so I could speak with them while they were still safely in their undersea prison. I was the last person they wanted to talk to. But I pulled out all the stops, and I brought all the charm. I mean *all* of it. I wove so many fairy tales you'd think I was the Brothers Grimm. And I was *great*! I made up a saga for the ages! A true Greek tragedy! I told them Zeus made me do it! I laid it on thick, and those dumb brutes lapped it up like Cerberus eating a soul trying to escape the Underworld. It wasn't nearly as dangerous a mission as I had expected. It was easy. Almost too easy.

Excited that everything was coming together, I

decided to check in with the other Hades. I wanted to see how things were going in the Underworld. I had asked him to recruit some of the nastier creatures to join our side of the battle, and I wanted to see how that was coming along and let him know we could count on the Titans. The other Hades and I had decided it was safest to use the magic mirrors the Odd Sisters had given us. Their magic was on a different frequency than the magic in my realm, and there was no chance anyone on Olympus would be tapping in. I summoned him the way Lucinda had taught me.

"Show me Hades in the Underworld!"

The other Hades appeared, his head flaming red, and Pain and Panic were cowering in the background as several souls glided into the Underworld, causing the soul counter on the wall behind Hades to tick in succession.

"Things aren't going so well, I take it," I said, shaking my head and wondering what Pain and Panic had done to incur his wrath. I felt a little guilty to be happy I wasn't there dealing with those bumbling fools. It was bad enough the Fates popped in and out of the Many Kingdoms at will; I didn't know what I would do if I had to deal with Pain and Panic as well.

"Aren't going so well? AREN'T GOING SO WELL? Well, that's an understatement for the ages! These imbeciles didn't kill Hercules, and he still has godlike strength. That's how it's going down here!" He motioned to Pain and Panic, who were trying to inch their way out of my view.

"Remind me to smite them the next time I'm there!"

"Get in line! The planets will be aligned in a matter of weeks. And now we have to find a way to kill Hercules." The other me shot flames at the little devils, making them scatter out of the room.

"What are you talking about? We have almost eighteen years. There's plenty of time!"

It turned out that while I had only been in the Many Kingdoms for a handful of weeks at most, in my own realm almost eighteen years had gone by. It didn't make sense.

"I guess time flies when you're having ice-cream parties and decorating your new fortress! And don't forget your

CRUSHING GUILT! I'm sure that passes the time!"

"Don't act like I'm up here floating on clouds like a big old baby! I just tricked the Titans into blaming Zeus for everything, and they've agreed to fight on our side!" Now both of us were exploding into red flames, and I was scaring my wraith ravens. They scattered out the windows while the other Hades screamed at me from the magic mirror.

"Great! But none of it will matter if we don't find a way to kill Wonder Boy!"

"Then send the Hydra! She'll devour him!" I said. I must have gotten all the smarts when my string was split; I didn't understand why else the other Hades was just sitting in the Underworld blowing his top when he should have been sending every monster we knew after Hercules.

"Hercules already defeated her! But I've got our little Nutmeg on the case, and I am sure she will find his weakness."

"She's your little Nutmeg, not mine."

"I forgot; you only collect the souls of witches. Well, when you're done with your little tea party, why don't you

GET DOWN HERE WHERE YOU BELONG AND HELP ME?" The other Hades was now completely engulfed in flames, and I thought that I couldn't possibly look so ridiculous when *I* got angry.

"Fine, fine. I'll be there as soon as I can. You plot with Meg, and I'll round up some of our friends when I get there. We'll throw everything we have at him! Medusa, a griffin, the Minotaur, all of them!"

I scrawled a note to Pflanze letting her know I was going to be gone for a while and to keep an eye on the sleeping dragon. Then I wiped the mirror quickly and called the Odd Sisters, but they weren't there. "Where are those dingbats?" I realized they probably didn't have a mirror on them. Instead, I hastily created a vortex so I could let them know I was going back to my realm to deal with stuff and would be back as soon as I could.

I saw the Odd Sisters in the small, round vortex, but they were not looking at me. I wasn't sure they were aware I was there on the other side, even though I kept calling their names. I couldn't tell what was going on. It was like a scene from an old horror movie.

I was half expecting Vincent Price to start narrating the gruesome scene, or Christopher Lee to pop out reciting one of his spooky monologues. The Odd Sisters were huddled in a dark basement with Gothel, surrounded by candles, and when one of them moved to the side, I saw they were standing over Primrose's and Hazel's dead bodies, and between them was a young girl who looked like she was under a sleeping curse. She had impossibly long golden hair that glowed in the darkness, and it was wrapped around the dead witches' bodies. The Odd Sisters' hands were bleeding, and the blood was dripping all over the sleeping girl and the dead witches as they chanted.

"Hey! Dingbats! Turn around!"

My voice startled them, making them spin in my direction.

"So this is what you're up to when you're away? Blood magic? I told you, it isn't safe."

The Odd Sisters looked like children who had been caught stealing candy, but their expressions quickly turned impish; their faces looked pale and frenzied from the magic they were doing.

"We're helping Gothel. Her sisters died, and we're trying to bring them back. You're the one who told us to make friends. This is what friends do," said Lucinda, smearing blood on her face as she pushed the hair out of her eyes.

"Who is that little girl? You know what, never mind, I don't have time to watch the sequel to *The Craft*! I'm taking a short trip to the Underworld to fulfill a cosmic prophecy. Please try not to get into any more trouble before I get back."

I was livid. It's not that I'm against necromancy; I've reanimated tons of dead people. It's pretty fun, actually. And it was none of my business if they wanted to put a princess under a sleeping curse and smear blood all over her. But there was something about the scene that just sent a chill through me, the same feeling I got when the Fates and Wraith Queens said the Odd Sisters would destroy the worlds when they found out who they really were. I had to wonder if I was right to send them on this path. I'd had no idea any of this would happen. I hadn't seen it in the Book of Fairy Tales when I read it, but I didn't have time to think about it, and I didn't have time for the Odd Sisters' antics. I'd have to talk with them when I got back. I just had to hope they didn't do any more damage in the meantime.

I made what I thought was a quick trip back to the Underworld to round up some of my old friends, like Medusa, the griffin, and the Minotaur. They all agreed to try to destroy Hercules, and I promised them places of honor in the new ruling pantheon if they succeeded. The other me was busy recruiting more monsters of his own and working with Meg by way of threats to see if she could find Hercules's weakness. I didn't know much about Meg, only that she had sold her soul to the other me and now she was one of his unwilling minions. It seemed like he and Meg had things covered, so I went back to the Many Kingdoms to check on the Odd Sisters. I was only away for a matter of days, but years had passed in the Many Kingdoms while I was gone. By the time I got back, the Odd Sisters had created a new Circe all on their own, without my help, and Maleficent had woken up and was squatting in my fortress, the Forbidden Mountain.

I had foolishly thought that since so much time had passed in the Underworld and Olympus while I had been in the Many Kingdoms, that meant almost no time at all would have passed in the Many Kingdoms while I was helping the other me. But it would seem that was not the case. It didn't make sense. And everything had gone terribly wrong. I saw it the moment I walked into the Odd Sisters' house.

The Odd Sisters were in the sitting room on the floor surrounded by piles of books, scraps of papers, candles, and jars of magical powders. They looked up, surprised to see me there.

"What are you doing here, demon?" Lucinda stood up, glaring at me. I could tell she wasn't the Lucinda I knew before I went away. There was something missing from inside her, like there was a vacant space, and in that space, something else, something putrid, was taking hold, and in my mind I saw it growing over time, and I knew it wasn't right. It was the oddest sensation, looking at my witches but not feeling like they were my witches anymore. They weren't themselves, and it sent that same chill through my body.

"What's happened to you? I was only gone for a few days; what have you done to yourselves?"

"You left us alone for years, Hades! You didn't keep your promise. We had to create Circe on our own!" said Lucinda.

"And we don't want you here when she gets back," said Ruby. "So leave!"

And in that moment, I knew what happened. They'd sacrificed themselves to make Circe. That was what was missing. They used the best parts of themselves to make her. And that pervasive evil, the legacy left by the Wraith Queens, was invading the empty spaces within them.

"We didn't sacrifice anything!" said Lucinda, reading my mind. "We gave her the best parts of us, and now we have our Circe again!"

"And we're going to do the same for Maleficent. She wants a daughter of her own, so we are going to share this gift with her," said Martha.

"You can't do that! It will kill her. Look what it's done to you!"

"What do you mean, Hades? What's wrong with

us?" asked Lucinda, her head tilted to one side, her eyes wide and vacant. I was heartbroken and completely taken aback by how altered they were. And it was my fault.

"You're not the same witches I once knew. You sacrificed too much of yourselves to create Circe; the spell will eat away at you as it did the witches in the Dead Woods, don't you see? And now you want to do the same to Maleficent? I won't let you!"

"What do you care about us? You left us here alone to fend for ourselves. Why shouldn't we help Maleficent? Give her a daughter to love, someone to care for, to live for, to protect?"

"This will ruin all of you. Don't you see, this is what the Fates said would happen. You must stop this now, before it's too late. You have to take back the parts of yourself used to create Circe."

"Take them back? That would kill her!" said the Odd Sisters, scratching at their faces and pulling their hair. They were going wild. I had never seen them like that. I rushed to them and tried to make them stop, but Lucinda took me off guard and sent me flying backward a few feet with her magic. I was surprised she was able to stop me. But that didn't matter. These were not my witches; they were not my delightful, and sometimes annoying, dingbats. They were something else.

"You would have us kill our own daughter?" Ruby was crying and ripping the lace from her dress into shreds.

"Yes, you have to! I will help you find a better way, a safe way to create another Circe, I promise. One that will not destroy you over time. One that won't shatter your souls. This is not safe magic."

"You're the one who told us to find the spell in the Dead Woods, and that is what we did! Now you're telling us it's dangerous. I think you're just jealous. You want us for yourself. You never liked Circe."

And in that moment my face appeared in all the Odd Sisters' mirrors. It was the other me, calling from the Underworld.

"Hercules defeated all of them! Every creature we sent after him. And our Meg can't seem to find his weakness, but I'm not sure she's telling the truth. I think they're falling in love."

Lucinda laughed. "It seems you have found his weakness," she said, and all the mirrors went blank. "There is nothing here for you, Hades. You abandoned your fortress to Maleficent, and you turned your back on us, leaving us here to fend for ourselves, and now you insult our magic and tell us to kill our own daughter? You never cared for us. You were never our family!" The house shook violently with her anger.

"That's not true, you dingbat; I'm trying to help you." I have to be honest here: I was pretty heart-broken. I couldn't believe I'd let this happen, and I decided if I had to, I would kill the new Circe myself and bring back the old one. I couldn't stand seeing my witches this way, and I knew I was to blame.

"Go back to the Underworld and rot. Your throne is empty and waiting for you."

I had never seen a look like that on Lucinda's face, not when talking to me, anyway. I had lost her. I had lost the Odd Sisters, and it hurt me more than losing my own brother.

"What are you talking about?"

"You did what you do best. You left the other

Hades to fight the battle alone, and he died in the river of death."

"You're insane. I literally just talked to him!"

"Do you honestly think after locking up Cronus, *the God of Time*, so many years ago, and *then* agreeing to release lesser Titans, that time would ever be on your side?"

I never thought I would hate the sound of Lucinda's laughter, but it felt like jagged shards of glass being plunged into my heart. "I don't believe you, witch!"

"Then see for yourself. It's right there in the Book of Fairy Tales." She waved her hand, and the book flew across the room. It landed with a thump right next to me and opened to a page that had my name on it. It was right there. *My story!*

"I didn't see this story when I read the Book of Fairy Tales!"

"It was still being written," said Lucinda, smiling at me in a way that made me think she wasn't sharing the entire story. She wasn't the witch I loved anymore. And she hated me because she thought I had abandoned her. Everything was spinning out of control; it was madness and chaos and falling into ruin. Just as it was fated.

"I have read tons of stories in this damnable book that haven't happened yet!" I said. I didn't understand what was going on, and Lucinda didn't seem willing to share the secrets of her precious book. I lost my temper.

"Look, witches, I loved you once, and gods help me, I may still, but you're walking a dangerously fine line. I'm going to give you a chance to tell me what's going on, but you know as well as I do that I can take you back to the Underworld in an instant and there won't be a thing you can do about it! So start talking!"

"We can't read the stories about ourselves until all the events completely unfold, *most of the time.* Sometimes we can see them as they are being written, sometimes we can't. Which seems to be the case with your tale. Look, there is still more to the story, something even we can't see. It seems our fates will be forever entangled, and only time will reveal how."

This didn't seem possible. "This is insanity!" I

said. But I sat there and read the rest of my own story in the Book of Fairy Tales—at least, everything that had been written—and I was shocked.

The other Hades made a deal with Hercules to give up his powers for twenty-four hours in exchange for Meg's soul. Good thinking, but it obviously didn't work. Lucinda was right. Meg was Hercules's weakness, and like all lovestruck fools, Hercules agreed, only to find out she had been working with the other me all along. After the deal was struck, the other Hades took off in his winged chariot. And let me say, that chariot was awesome! It had black leathery wings on each side and a wicked face, and it was pulled by a giant black dragon with red eyes. The planets aligned just as the Fates had decreed, and a dark beam of light shot down from the cosmos onto the very place where the other Hades would find the Titans. Everything was going according to plan. Except I wasn't there. I was supposed to be there! This was *my* battle, *my* master plan, everything I had worked for! All I could do was read about it, as the waters of the sea parted and the vault was revealed. The other Hades called down to the Titans. He was commanding and magnificent to behold.

"Brothers! Titans! Look at you in this squalid prison. Who put you down there?" he yelled.

"Zeus!" the Titans called out.

"And now that I set you free, what is the first thing you're going to do?" His voice was deep, villainous, and imbued with his dark intentions.

"Destroy him!" the Titans rumbled.

One by one the colossal Titans marched toward Olympus, all except Cyclops. The other Hades sent him off to kill Hercules. A brilliant plan! A plan that should have worked. Hercules was human now, vulnerable; everything was in our favor. There was no way Hercules could win a fight against a Titan without his godlike strength. Except he did. All because of a technicality. A technicality! Something about the deal he made with the other Hades, some stupid thing about no harm coming to Meg, and when she got hurt, well, the deal was off, and Hercules got his powers back. Meanwhile, the other me was sitting on the throne on Olympus, sipping honey wine out of a glass with an umbrella in it like a fool, while the Lurker and the Lord of Flame encased Zeus in hardened lava. And who shows up but Hercules, just as the Fates said he might, and the rest is history. Or myth, or however you choose to look at it. For me, it was a defeat.

The looks on the Odd Sisters' faces as I read the Book of Fairy Tales told me it was all true. I saw everything in my mind's eye as I read the Book of Fairy Tales, almost as if I were watching the events in one of the Odd Sisters' magic mirrors. I wish I had been—maybe I could have helped, stopped it, changed the course of destiny. But there was nothing, nothing I could do when I saw Hercules ride into the Underworld on *my dog* and knock the other me into the river of death, sealing my fate.

I failed. I failed the other Hades, I failed myself, and I failed the Odd Sisters. It seemed *that* was my fate. Just as it was my fate to take the throne in the Underworld again. But that was not the end of my story. As the Odd Sisters said, my story was still being written.

CHAPTER XIII

A CHANGE OF FATE

The Book of Fairy Tales had stopped playing, but as Hades said, his story was not over. It was still being written. Dark clouds were gathering over the Dead Woods now, illuminated by flashing bolts of red lightning that penetrated the stone walls of the mansion, causing them to crack and crumble. The sky was red with blood, and the stone angels in the Dead Woods were weeping, just as the Fates had warned. The room was shaking, causing everything on the table to rattle, the dishes clattering and cups falling over. Everyone looked around, wondering what was happening, and then they saw it—the stone dragon's head in the fireplace was moving. It had come to life, twisting its head right to left, cracking the stone. The fireplace collapsed, freeing the dragon from its imprisonment.

Everyone scattered from the dining table right before the dragon slammed into it, and the table broke into piles of jagged stone. The dragon jumped onto the low wall, knocking over the candles and taking out one of the pillars as it spread its long wings and took off soaring into the sky.

The mansion was shaking so violently that pieces of stone were falling from the ceiling as the creatures that were carved into the stone building were coming to life, one by one, smashing their ways out of the windows and taking to the sky to join the dragon. The party rushed to the window to see what was happening. The stone ravens, gargoyles, and harpies were in flight. Even the weeping angels were imbued with life and were now circling above the Dead Woods as the dead emerged from their graves, marching toward the mansion.

Hades looked around, trying to find the source

of the magic, the person or thing causing this. He made his mind still and felt for the vibrations of the entities responsible, but they were eluding him. They were hiding in the shadows, like the insidious witches they were, and then he knew in that moment who it was: the Odd Sisters.

"This is my fault!" Circe cried. "I should have never tried to fuse my mothers into one person. We were happy in the Place Between. But I was selfish and wanted my mother with me in the land of the living, here in the Dead Woods. I thought combining them would make that possible."

"You did what was fated, Circe. You're not meant to be in the Place Between. Just like I wasn't meant to stay in the Many Kingdoms," said Hades.

"So you're meant to be the lord of the Underworld, forever doomed to be alone? For the record, I would happily help you destroy Zeus, if you asked me. I almost destroyed your other brother for what he did to Ursula," said Circe, making Hades smile. He loved seeing flashes of Lucinda within her.

"Don't take this the wrong way, but you really do have the best parts of your mothers," he said. "Neither of us can escape our fates, Circe."

"She is nothing like us!" The Odd Sisters' voices penetrated the entire mansion, making it rumble more violently than before, causing more stones to crash down around them. Hades heard their screeches coming from the library, and the group ran to see what was happening.

There, they saw the Odd Sisters, making their way through the portrait hanging over the fireplace. Clawing their way out. They looked like giant insects, their bodies contorting and squeezing out from the tight space, skittering down the stone walls until finally they were standing before them. Lucinda looked as if she had been torn apart and haphazardly stitched back together again. Blood oozed from the great gashes in her face as she laughed uncontrollably. The faces of Ruby and Martha were also soaked in blood, their eyes peering at Hades and the younger witches, radiating pain, terror, and hatred.

Even Hades was horrified, and he ruled the dead. He searched their faces, trying to find something of the witches he loved, but the witches he loved were no longer within them, and something truly horrible had taken their place. It broke his heart to see them this way.

"Oh, Lucinda, my dearest witch. Who did this to you? Why didn't you use your magic to heal your wounds?" he asked, touching the deep gashes in her face tenderly.

"I wanted Circe to see what she did to me. I am in torment. You know Circe must die. You thought about doing it yourself, years ago. It's the only way to end this, the only way to have us back."

"Ah, my loves," he said, looking at the Odd Sisters. He knew he owed this to them. He knew he had to make it right. Circe would understand.

CHAPTER XIV

HAPPILY EVER AFTERLIFE

Hades was back home in the Underworld after his ordeal in the Dead Woods, drinking pomegranate wine on the terrace and watching the ferryman usher in the dead. He had grown to love this view of the river Styx and made it his nightly ritual to watch as the dead first set foot on the shores of the Underworld. But this evening he was awaiting the new arrivals with even more anticipation than usual. He watched as they stepped off the boat, each of them giving the ferryman a coin before disembarking and making their way to his fortress, where he had a lavish banquet waiting for them.

Hades had spent many evenings this way, trying to content himself with the company of the dead, and this evening was no different. He saw his new guests coming, making their way up the winding path that led to his palace, and he got up and walked to the dining room so he could greet the dead before their feast, as was his custom. This evening there would be fewer guests in attendance than usual, but Hades didn't mind. He heard the sound of their clicking heels on the onyx floors and knew they were almost there.

And then he saw them, his witches, his Lucinda, Ruby, and Martha, looking exactly as they had the first night he met them.

"Welcome back, witches!" he said, smiling at them. Their sweet laughter rang throughout the halls of the Underworld as they called his name and ran to greet him, hugging him over and over and covering his cheeks with their red lip paint.

"So I take it you've forgiven me for killing you?" he asked, pouring them some wine and handing them their glasses.

"You've made us whole again. You saved Circe, and you saved us. Of course we forgive you."

"Thank the deities," he said, spying himself in his magic mirror. "I look like Jack Burton!" he said as he wiped the lip paint from his face. He knew the Odd Sisters had no idea who he was talking about, but it didn't matter. He was happy to be with his witches again, to be laughing with them and making jokes they didn't understand. "And because I know you're going to ask: Circe is fine, and so are Primrose, Hazel, and Jacob. They're working to restore the Dead Woods," said Hades, fending off more kisses and hugs.

"What about the Wraith Queens? Do Circe, Primrose, and Hazel know how to protect themselves from them?" Lucinda had only been herself again for a matter of hours, and she was already fretting over Circe. Hades was pleased.

"Oh, I banished those hags. I should have done it hundreds of years ago. But enough of that. I have a surprise for you—well, two surprises, actually,"

Hades said, beaming with both of his hands up, his fingers wiggling excitedly.

"Is that our surprise? Pizzazz hands?" asked Martha, rolling her eyes.

"No, you dingbat! But they're great, right?" he said, cracking himself up again. "This surprise is even better than pizzazz hands, if you can believe it! BEHOLD!" he said, stretching out his arm like a carnival barker might when presenting a major attraction.

"Circe!" the Odd Sisters screamed, running toward her. "What are you doing here?" And then they stopped, realizing who it was. This wasn't their daughter; it was their sister. The Circe who had been taken away from them so many years before. They just stood there, looking at her, until they were overcome with joy, covering her in kisses and hugging her again and again.

"Isn't anyone going to say hello to me?" It was Pflanze.

The Odd Sisters gasped, rushing over and fawning over her, giving her kisses and scrinches behind her ears. "How did you get here, you wicked cat?" asked Lucinda, picking her up.

"Pflanze has been with me for a while now," said Hades, scratching her under her chin. "It's only fitting that the great Hecate take her place in the Underworld where she belongs." Hades smiled at them, flashing his dagger teeth and brilliant yellow eyes.

"That was our secret, Hades!" said Pflanze, eyeing him.

"Oh, come on, we're all family here. And it's not like they wouldn't guess once Circe eventually sees fit to change you back into your real form," he said cheekily.

"What's this? What's going on?" said the Odd Sisters as one. They had no idea what Hades was talking about.

"Everyone, calm down. We can talk about it over dinner. And look, I had my minions put out my finest bone china," he said, cracking himself up and filling their skull chalices with more wine. "Get it? *Bone china?*"

This time the Odd Sisters got the joke, and they

all ended up on the floor laughing, dropping their chalices and spilling their wine.

"Let's make a toast," Hades said, handing them each a new chalice. "To family." He held up his chalice with one hand while petting Pflanze with the other. "To Circe, to Hecate, and to my little Furies! May we all live deliciously."

Hades was happy, happier than he had ever been, and he wondered if they deserved such a delicious ending, but he didn't care. He finally had laughter in the Underworld again. His witches were home at last.

EPILOGUE

Circe, Primrose, and Hazel stood in their courtyard, looking up at the dark curtain of night scattered with twinkling stars. Most of the dead had gone back to their resting places, along with the statues that had come to life when Lucinda laid siege to the Dead Woods. Even the stone dragon was now back in its place, and Jacob was resting in his crypt. They were all exhausted, and the Dead Woods were quiet once more, thanks to Hades. The queens almost missed having him there, and they wondered if he would visit them again. It seemed the chaos had finally ended for the ladies of the Dead Woods. Hades had taken Lucinda, Ruby, and Martha with him to the

Underworld and banished the Wraith Queens, who would never haunt their kingdom again. And it seemed to Circe, Primrose, and Hazel that they were truly free to make the Dead Woods as they wanted, effecting real change in the Many Kingdoms. From this point they would be writing the Book of Fairy Tales, and they would make up for what the previous queens and the Odd Sisters had done during their reigns of terror.

They made their way back inside the mansion, inspecting every room to make sure they had repaired all the damage, until finally they reached the solarium, where tea and cookies were waiting for them. They sat and drank their tea, chatting about what had happened, each of them feeling like everything was different now. They knew the Odd Sisters would never return, at least not in madness or in terror.

"Looks like Hades forgot his teacup! I bet it's because he wants an excuse to come back," said Primrose, laughing. Even though she was as tired as her sister and Circe, she knew sleep wouldn't come for and Ruby and Martha are still inside her, but that story hasn't happened yet. What's even weirder is that you reference the breaking of the worlds, but it seemed like something *we* had to fix, not Hades. What does that mean?"

"I think it means Hades changed fate. Perhaps we do have the power to change our fates, if only a little. And thank the gods, because I couldn't think of a happier ending for Hades and my mothers," said Circe, smiling at Primrose and Hazel.

"Do you realize what's happened? We actually changed events in the Book of Fairy Tales. That's incredible," said Primrose. She was happier than she'd ever been. And she wondered if it would be possible to change the fates of others. Only time would tell.

Just then, a raven flew through an open window with a scroll tied to her little foot. The bird perched on the table near the window, eyeing the plate of cherry-and-almond cookies sitting there among the tea things. She hopped impatiently and then held out her little foot for one of them to take the scroll.

"Oh, it must be from Snow!" said Primrose,

taking the note from the raven. "Thank you," she said to the bird, patting her on the head and giving her a cookie after she let out a soft caw. The raven ate the cookie and flew out the window, cawing to the ravens and crows perched in the trees in the courtyard.

"What does it say?" asked Circe.

Primrose looked pale and frightened.

"Snow White needs our help. Something is wrong with Grimhilde's mirror. She needs us to come right away."

And in that moment, Primrose, Circe, and Hazel knew they were truly the new trio of witches in this land. They would be a new sort of Odd Sisters. They would be the Ladies of Light, just as Hades said.

THE END